Y0-BQR-168

Bubba, Missy & Me

Also by Eugene Platt:

coffee and solace (poems)
Six of One / Half Dozen of the Other (with John Tomikel)
Allegheny Reveries
A Patrick Kavanagh Anthology (Ed.)
an original sin
Don't Ask Me Why I Write These Things (Ed.)
The Turnings of Autumn (Ed.)
Metamorphosis (Ed.)
South Carolina State Line
Coffee and Solace (a novel-in-progress)

Bubba, Missy & Me

Excerpted from *Coffee and Solace*,
a Novel-in-Progress

by Eugene Platt

Tradd Street Press
Charleston, South Carolina

Published by Tradd Street Press
38 Tradd Street
Charleston, SC 29401

Disclaimer: This is a work of fiction. All names, characters, incidents, and places are either figments of the author's imagination or used fictitiously. Opinions expressed and attitudes exhibited are the characters' and are not necessarily the author's.

Acknowledgments

Portions of this book appeared in *Omnibus*, which published an earlier version of "Nunc Dimittis" under the title "Eye of the Storm," and *Jubilate Deo*, which published part of "Communion" under the title "Priscilla and Bubba."

Excerpt from *Saint Joseph Daily Missal*, copyright © 1959, 1961, Catholic Book Publishing Corp., New York, N.Y. All rights reserved. Used by permission.

Material from *The Book of Common Prayer* (Episcopal) is in the public domain. The Church Hymnal Corporation, New York, N.Y., is thanked for confirming its status.

Poem "The Grieving" is from the collection *Walking on Water* by Mario A. Petaccia. Copyright © 1986 by Mario A. Petaccia. Used by permission.

Poems from the collection *South Carolina State Line* by Eugene Platt. Copyright © 1980 by Eugene Platt.

Special thanks to the Rev. Alanson Houghton, the Rev. Arthur Jenkins, Robert Moran, M.D., and the Rev. William Rhett, Jr., Ed.D., for reading and critiquing portions of the manuscript; to Constance Pultz for editorial and proofreading assistance; to Vanessa Cramer for help with proofreading as well as generously donating much of the typesetting; to Kathleen Ellis for editing and proofreading assistance; to The Citadel Writing Center for "Grammar Hotline" help; to David Hamilton of Tradd Street Press; to my daughter and son, Troye and Paul Platt, for critiquing the manuscript and their early encouragement; and to my wife Mary, whose loving support was the equivalent of a major grant from NEA and without which it is unlikely this book could have been written.

Designed and typeset by Vanessa Cramer Design.
The text typeface is 12 pt. Bookman. Headings and titles are Caslon 540 Italic.
Printed by Furlong Printing Co., Charleston, S.C. on recycled paper.

Library of Congress Catalog Card Number: 92-64263
ISBN 0-937684-29-5

Foreword

Pleased as I have been many Monday nights in recent years to help serve spaghetti as a volunteer at the homeless shelter sponsored by the Charleston Interfaith Crisis Ministry, I have also wanted to help CICM, as well as the Star Gospel Mission, *through my writing.* An opportunity presented itself in the context of *Coffee and Solace*, a novel I began writing in July 1991 and may well be working on for another year or longer. Someone suggested that selected passages from this novel-in-progress could make for a very readable book in itself. Thus, *Bubba, Missy & Me* was conceived.

Given the charitable dimension of this project, it is hoped readers will be charitable themselves regarding any shortcomings to which excerpted works tend to be susceptible. It is also hoped that these good readers will wait patiently to learn more about *"Bubba, Missy & Me"* in *Coffee and Solace.*

Eugene Platt
July 1992

for

Arthur Jenkins

with

appreciation, admiration, and agape

Contents

Discovery
13

Miracle on Savage Road
25

Boys and Bridges
36

Missy & Me
48

The USC Knights
56

A Room of Her Own
65

Wedding
70

Separation
79

Santa Fe
88

Communion
102

Dinner
112

Nunc Dimittis
125

Discovery

Bubba Brinson was my best friend. His real name, alas, was Middleton Jackson Brinson, a family legacy such as many boys in the South are saddled with by well-meaning parents. He was so well liked by his peers, however, we gave him the nickname in compassion for what was to us the stilted sound of the other. He loved it. "Bubba," as a term of endearment, came to represent him and became part of him a long time before its unfortunate stereotyping. *Our* Bubba was a great wit, but the term "buffoon" did not aptly describe him. As far as I know, he was never inclined to discard his nickname; neither am I so inclined in referring to someone so dear to me.

Bubba's family lived not far from mine in that region of Charleston lying on the west side of the Ashley River, which separates it from the old city. (The oldest part of the city is sequestered on a peninsula bordered by the Ashley and Cooper Rivers, which, according to local wits, come together at its tip to form the Atlantic Ocean.) When he and I were growing up, where we lived was generally known as St. Andrew's Parish. Residents of the region, which encompassed a wide variety of neighborhoods, tended to have strong affinities with each other and shared a deep parochial pride. In part, that pride came from having an outstanding public school system, thriving churches whose membership included almost everyone, and natural beauty continually enhanced by the planting of countless thousands of camellias and azaleas and other shrubs and flowers by successive generations of St. Andrew's residents.

Although "St. Andrew's Parish" was a sonorous name, some pragmatic real estate people evidently found this colonial ecclesiastical designation too sectarian or otherwise too cumbersome for business and changed it to a utilitarian "West of the Ashley." Eventually they shortened it to "West Ashley." It is unlikely that this name-tampering was instigated by natives; more likely it was done sneakily by latter-day carpetbaggers, geriatric transplants, and other immigrants from "off," a melting-pot mixture of people from Snow Belt places like New York (which I heard shortened its own name from New Amsterdam because two syllables were better for business than four), Newark, Detroit, Youngstown, Chicago, Pittsburgh, places where the preservation of names as well as other traditions has a lower priority than is the custom in Charleston. In any case, I never got used to the change. It was as if my own given name had been changed without my concurrence.

Specifically, the Brinsons lived in Avondale, one of the nicer St. Andrew's subdivisions, one in which most of the houses were built of stone or brick and bigger than ours. Of course, the Brinsons were expected to live well: they were Episcopalians. In fact, Mrs. Brinson's uncle, Matthew Middleton Jackson, was Bishop of the Episcopal Diocese of South Carolina. Mr. Brinson was one of the Brinsons in Brinson, Middleton, Morris, Brinson and Brinson, a prominent law firm on Broad Street.

To my father, his good friend William Brinson would always be known as "Billy Bugle." The nickname was a lighthearted reference to their college days at The Citadel, where the two had been classmates. In those days, as an assigned duty, Mr. Brinson roused the corps of cadets every morning by sounding reveille on his bugle. While his performances were noteworthy, they were not particularly popular with his fellow cadets. This motivational music would have made Billy Bugle a pariah among them if it were not for the fact that he was an outstanding player on the school's football team, the Bulldogs, as well as a member of its tennis team and captain of the new sailing club.

(The Citadel, of course, is a military college in Charleston or, as some alumni prefer to express it, *The* Military College of South Carolina. A few partisans even

seem to think it is one of the last remaining strongholds of the Confederacy. In fact, the Confederate Stars and Bars is flown prominently over the campus beside the Stars and Stripes and the state flag.

Be that as it may, many historians do credit The Citadel's cadets with initiating hostilities in the Civil War when they fired on a Union ship attempting to resupply Fort Sumter. It is also notable that, soon after South Carolina's secession, the entire corps of cadets volunteered for military service with the new Confederacy.

More recently, this "West Point of the South" received an additional measure of fame, or infamy, when one of its alumni wrote a novel that was made into a movie portraying its resident racism, hazing, and so forth. Naturally, college officials trying to protect their institutional image denied permission to producers of the film to shoot it on The Citadel campus. Unfortunately, controversies involving allegations of racism and hazing continue to crop up occasionally, tending to tarnish the school's "spit and polish" luster.)

Bubba was only a month older than I, although in terms of worldliness he was years ahead of me. We looked a lot alike, both of us towheads who could have been cousins. We were about the same height and weight, were about equally strong, and had had similar grades at St. Andrew's Elementary School. We even had similar bicycles and other trappings of childhood. In fact, Bubba had only one thing I did not and really envied, a sister.

Being with other children at least part of almost every day was no substitute for the sibling I always wanted and never had. For a child there is no substitute for sharing living space with another child. Perfect parents or privileges might compensate, but again, there is no substitute. Unconsciously I permitted loneliness to personify itself and adopted it as a surrogate brother. With a perverse loyalty, its vestiges would be my lifelong companion.

One hot July afternoon when it was too sticky to play baseball or do much of anything else, Bubba and I were lounging in hammocks in his shady back yard, sipping lemonade and talking about the extraordinary season the Charleston Rebels were having. We were thirteen that summer, but as Bubba's mother liked to say, he was "going on twenty-one."

The Brinsons' back yard was a wonderful place for a boy to be. On one side was a paved tennis court; on the other was an open lawn large enough for the pickup games of baseball or football we played according to the season. In between on a brick patio were a permanent barbecue grill, redwood tables, and benches. Every year during the season, usually from late September until early April—those months having the letter *r* in their names, the Brinsons hosted a number of oyster roasts in their back yard to which my family was always invited.

There was no swimming pool because, as Mr. Brinson always calmly pointed out whenever his wife suggested it would be nice to have one, with all the beaches around Charleston none was needed. Besides, they were privileged to own a large, cedar-shingled second home on the front beach on Sullivan's Island. This beautiful beach house had been in Mrs. Caroline Middleton Brinson's family for several generations. It was affectionately known as "Middleton Manor" and the Brinsons stayed there almost every weekend from early May through Labor Day.

The far reaches of the yard sloped down to the wide marsh on the west side of the Ashley River. Weeping willow and palmetto trees grew in low places along the edge of the marsh and afforded a sense of privacy without blocking too much of the river view.

The marsh itself was a haven for a wide variety of wildlife. Wading birds fed and nested there, and occasionally were meals themselves for roving raccoons. The smell of the marsh was unique, almost impossible to describe to anyone who has never inhaled it. Simultaneously, it seemed to be sweet and sour, pleasant and pungent. On dark nights, the marsh teemed not only with wildlife of the real world, but also with the creatures of our fantasies.

A tributary, just barely wide enough and deep enough at high tide for Mr. Brinson's small sailboat,

connected the yard to the river. We christened the tributary "Crustacean Creek" in honor of all the crabs we caught there. In practice, naturally, it was always called "Crab Creek" in honor of all the crustaceans. The manner of the christening ceremony, I'm sorry to say, may have been inappropriate.

On many occasions Bubba and I camped out in that back yard, sleeping in a tent close to the marsh. We would build a small fire for hot dogs and later roast marshmallows over the coals. Inevitably one of us quipped, "Marshmallows are good for marsh fellows," and before settling in the tent for the night one of us usually announced he had to go "rechristen the creek." Bubba would smuggle one or two of his special magazines from his room and by flashlight we would look at the pictures of naked women until we fell asleep.

Sometimes we were awakened in the middle of the night by exotic sounds coming from the marsh or from the zoo across the river at Hampton Park, sometimes by a train crossing the Seaboard Railroad trestle a mile or so upstream. On Saturday mornings during the school year we awoke to the martial music of a bugle playing reveille at The Citadel, whose campus was right across the river from us.

We joked that the bugler was the ghost of a boy who died and became Mr. Brinson. Often, upon awaking we were awestruck by the sight of the sun seeming to rise out of the river. Afterwards, we usually crawled back into our sleeping bags for another hour or two. We were sure our routine was better than the regimen of the Boy Scouts—and never were we inclined to follow in our fathers' footsteps, passing through The Citadel's guarded gates to don its uniforms and its discipline!

Anyhow, on that particular sticky summer afternoon already mentioned, Bubba and I were arguing about whether Savannah or Jacksonville would be the Rebels' strongest opponent that season. We had just decided we needed more lemonade when Mrs. Brinson came out of the house calling, "Bubba, I have to run to the Piggly Wiggly to get something for supper. Missy's reading. Don't harass her while I'm gone. If you and Andy want more lemonade, there's a fresh pitcher inside. There's also a tray of brownies cooling on top of the stove. Help yourselves but don't make a mess."

"Thanks, Mom. And not to worry—we'll have Missy clean up the mess," Bubba responded.

"I'll be back in about an hour. If your father gets home first, tell him where I've gone, O.K.?"

"O.K., Mom. *¡Vaya con Dios!*"

When Mrs. Brinson had backed her big navy blue Chrysler out of the driveway onto Arcadian Way, Bubba hopped up saying, "Caroline's never back in less than two hours. She'll run into a friend in the produce section at the Pig who'll tell her about bananas being two cents less at Rodenberg's or the A & P, and she'll go there too. Come on inside, Andy. Got something to show you."

I followed with some uneasiness, guessing Bubba had a new magazine hidden under his mattress. I had long since promised Jesus (when He had spared my dog's life, an incident I shall relate later) that I would not look at those pictures of naked women anymore, and I was loath to break any promise to Him. Of course, that was not the kind of information I shared with Bubba. He would not have been impressed. In fact, he often teased by calling me "John," code for John the Baptist.

My emotions were mixed as we crossed the lawn. I felt I had to feign disinterest, but actually was curious. At the same time, I felt concern at the prospect of breaking a sacred promise. I said, "Man, I hope you're not planning to bore me with more of your magazines. See one pair of naked tits, you've seen them all."

Bubba retorted, "Relax, Andy. No titty magazines. Something better."

Entering the kitchen, we paused to fill a plate with brownies and to refill our glasses. As he opened the refrigerator, Bubba jested, "Would we rather have a couple of my dad's beers? A couple of Buds would go well with the entertainment I've got lined up for us." I just grinned and he added, "Oh, I forgot, 'John,' you're Baptist. We'll just have to stick with the lemonade and pretend it's gin and tonic."

I noticed Missy in the adjacent family room. She was

stretched out on the floor, reading a book, and apparently oblivious to us. As discreetly as possible, I glanced in her direction several times. She was eleven, freckled and slender, angelic in some inarticulable way, and, to me, already as covetable as a perfect peach.

On several occasions my parents had "made" me go with them to see Missy perform in her dance school's annual recitals. For the sake of my already machismo-tainted image, I guess, I felt as if I had to protest, but secretly I enjoyed watching the dancers. Ironically, while we Baptists were permitted with impunity to enjoy ballet, either as participants or as spectators, ballroom dancing was frowned upon. I would never understand this apparent inconsistency but would always be glad the South Carolina and Southern Baptist Conventions allowed it. Early on, I began to develop an appreciation for this most sensual of art forms I would never lose.

Missy was wearing white summer shorts that day, and a green tee shirt. As usual she was barefooted. Already there were budding breasts barely discernible beneath her shirt. "Bubba's a lucky devil," I was thinking, "to live in the same house with a creature like her!"

I had always been intrigued by the opposite sex. Even in early childhood I perceived girls to be somehow mysteriously different. I never wanted to be one—the very idea of being without a boy's prerogatives was unnerving. Nevertheless, had I been an only female child, I probably would have found little boys to be similarly mysterious and coveted a brother.

I followed Bubba into his bedroom, the walls of which were decorated with posters, pennants from New York, Washington, D.C., and other places he had visited on family vacations, as well as newspaper clippings concerning the Rebels and other South Atlantic League baseball teams. There was also the souvenir program from a New York Yankee game the family had seen earlier in the summer. It was an interesting, spacious room with windows on two sides.

Bubba pulled down all the window shades and switched on a rotating red light that reminded me of those on police cars. (This was a long time before they began using blue.) He said, "Close the door, Andy, and sit on the bed. We don't have very long. You're about to see something only real men get to see. Ready to become a real man?"

I snapped back, "I'm as much of a man as you. What are you talking about?"

"Just sit still and relax. You'll see in a minute." He turned on his phonograph, which had a record of jazz music already set to play. Then he opened the door and called, "Missy, we're ready." Bubba looked at me with a mischievous grin and before I could say anything Missy was standing in the doorway. Bubba closed the door behind her and sat beside me on his bed. "On with the show," he directed and, as easily as if she had rehearsed this performance for months, Missy began swaying her slender hips and writhing to the music.

This is fun, I thought, but what did Bubba mean about "something only real men get to see"? Then, as if she had been reading my mind, Missy eased her tee shirt high enough to bare her navel. In it a small piece of costume jewelry sparkled in the rotating red light. This was titillating, but I had to show Bubba I was remaining calm, so I said, "That's a nice navel—sort of like a third eye—which reminds me, did you know that Eve had no navel?"

Bubba just replied, "Pay attention, Andy. There's more to come."

Now Missy's back was turned to us as she slowly continued to raise her shirt. I *was* paying close attention. With her back still turned to us, she pulled the shirt completely off and tossed it over her head. I fully expected her next movement would be to dart out the door, but she continued to dance. A moment later I was startled when she turned around, exposing to us her uncovered breasts. With widening eyes, I stared at the strawberry-sized breasts with their darker, tiny cranberrylike nipples, which, like another pair of eyes, stared back. My jaw dropped, my heart raced. I ceased to be conscious of the jazz.

Bubba said, "You're doing fine, Missy. Now, act two."

Then, still moving to the music, the performer unzipped her shorts, letting them slide tantalizingly down the full length of her long-for-her-age legs. She lifted her left foot from the shorts and with the right flicked them aside. It was amazing—dancing just ten feet from my face was a live girl wearing only panties! But don't ask me whether they were white or pink, lacy or plain—my mind was spellbound by the body moving in front of me.

The music was building toward a climax now, and Missy's movements remained synchronized. Hooking her thumbs over the top of her panties, she pulled them down to her ankles. As with the shorts, she lifted her left foot first, and with the right flicked them aside. The music ended.

I was stunned, barely hearing Bubba call to her, "O.K., Missy, you've got the part!" Without looking at us, Missy had snatched up her clothes and already left the room. I continued to stare into the space where she had performed. The red light continued to rotate.

Bubba stood up, turned out the light, and raised the window shades. "Well, my man, what do you think of that?" he asked.

My best friend had just exposed me to a totally new experience, one of the most exciting of my life, but I could think of nothing manly to say. I turned and saw he was grinning at me, awaiting an appropriate reply. I said, "That's great jazz, Bubba, and I like your light." I paused while groping for an exit line, then added, "Well, I need to get home now. My mom said we're having an early supper and I've got to cut some grass first." Outside, mounting my bicycle, I was still preoccupied but remembered to mention the refreshments. "And thanks a lot for the gin and tonic," I said.

Bubba replied, "Anytime, old man—by the way, you're right about Eve not having a navel. Of course, I don't suppose Adam had one either."

"They were a wild couple, weren't they?" I said. "I wonder if, after they started wearing the fig leaves, Missy ever did a striptease for Adam."

"If *who* ever did a striptease for Adam?"

"I mean Eve," I said, blushing with embarrassment

for having exposed the object of my distraction.

Bubba laughed at my Freudian slip, then asked, "But, surely, 'John,' you don't believe Adam and Eve were real people, do you?"

"My Sunday School teacher does. I'm not sure," I answered before pedaling off with what was a standard farewell of those days, "Got to get going. See ya later, 'gator."

At bedtime that night, I went through the usual routine: brushed my teeth, did the daily Bible reading decreed in Nashville, mecca of Southern Baptists, and turned out the light. In the dim moonlight, kneeling beside my bed, I must have mumbled a prayer, but my mind was still stuck in Bubba's room. I crawled between the cool sheets and lay there not the least bit sleepy, quite conscious of my first erection of which I have any memory.

I remained wide awake, my eyes wide open in the warm darkness. Hours seemed to pass as I lay there mesmerized by Missy's image. It did not appear that the attendant hardness pushing up the sheet would ever subside sufficiently to let me sleep. I tried to think of other things, like baseball, the Rebels' game with the Indians Daddy and I planned to see on Saturday, mowing our lawn for some spending money, the eerie noises of midsummer night floating through the open windows—but fantasies of cuddling with Missy could not be overcome so easily.

To redeem these fantasies, I tried to think of activities she and I could enjoy that were—well, proper, like going to the Avondale Drugstore for ice cream, going to the Charleston County Public Library and reading books together, later going to high school dances together, later still getting married and only then holding her in that special close way husbands are allowed to hold their wives.

The luminous hands on my clock indicated two a.m. and sleep was nowhere near. Finally, I was beginning to feel tired as well as frustrated. Suddenly, without forethought, my hand struck out to slap the offending organ. Every nerve in that part of my body tingled.

Something geyser-like began boiling in my lower abdomen. It moved slowly at first, then with the exhilarating speed of a roller coaster as it goes over the humps and races down. The head of my penis seemed to burst and I to be half-immersed in warm syrup. It was not unlike the warm feeling I had had all over upon being baptized at First Baptist Church several years earlier. For a moment I shall never forget, my whole being was magically transported into a realm of rapture, a state of new sensations.

While the event was totally unexpected, I had had enough birds-and-bees education from my peers to know what had happened. As significant to me as were discoveries of new worlds to the explorers of old, I had discovered masturbation.

Note, however, that just as almost every discovery of Columbus or other explorers can be termed a mixed blessing, so could my discovery of my own sexuality. Along with whatever was good about it, there would always be a counterbalance of guilt. That, too, was part of my Baptist heritage.

At some point in time after that accidental event, I felt compelled by needs I did not fully understand to give myself relief purposefully. There were hundreds of such instances before I graduated from high school without knowing (in the Biblical sense) a female even once. Like my peers, I sometimes sought that surrogate relief in bed, more often in the bathroom; unlike them, I always prayed for forgiveness afterward. Such is often the case when a Baptist boy is initiated into the brotherhood of Adam, exchanging as a rite of passage the wisdom of innocence for the knowledge of experience.

I got on my bicycle and went by to see Bubba at least several times a week the rest of that summer, hoping to be treated to a repeat of Missy's stellar performance. I tried to be nonchalant while coveting another look, a second bite of the apple, to taste again this forbidden fruit of Baptist boyhood.

Unfortunately (or fortunately, depending on your perspective), circumstances were never quite right for a repeat, a re-run. Over and over I kicked myself for not having had the presence of mind to ask Bubba for an encore at the one moment in time such may have been possible. Usually, the object of my preoccupation would be off visiting her friends or Mrs. Brinson would be home. On one occasion, Mrs. Brinson was out for the afternoon and Missy was home; but, right after I arrived, Ruth Smalls dropped by to visit Missy. Inasmuch as Ruth's father, like mine, was a deacon in our church, I could not even conjure a fantasy of her and Missy performing together.

Ironically, neither Bubba nor I ever mentioned the matter again. I suspected Missy had been embarrassed and informed her easygoing, sometimes overbearing brother in no uncertain terms that her stint as a stripper had ended.

Accordingly, in lieu of learned discussions on the subtleties of striptease and other erotic arts, Bubba and I talked about sports the rest of the summer. As for baseball, our Rebels won the pennant. Left fielder Hank Rourk hit fifty-one home runs, setting a league record and breaking five or six bats in the process. Seven players batted over .300. And as it happened, neither Savannah nor Jacksonville was runner-up; dark horse Augusta surprised everyone.

Miracle on Savage Road

One Saturday morning several years before the striptease incident, something remarkable happened which everyone who has ever heard it agrees is at least a good story. That quality alone, of course, would make it worthy of retelling. For me personally, however, the event has considerably more significance than just a good story. Surely, many of my subsequent acts and attitudes have confirmed it as a defining moment of my childhood.

Since I did not have to rush to get ready for school that day, I was waking up leisurely while waiting for the last call to breakfast. To be honest, I was slow to leave the womb-like comfort of my bed whenever I could. My top cover was a chenille spread, cherished because I always slept under it when visiting my grandparents' house and because my grandmother gave the spread to me when she finally had to move from that place to Enston Homes, a community for the elderly that looks like a Victorian village.

I was simultaneously trying to listen to some silly program (a Saturday morning serial, probably) on my bedside radio and to recall details of a dream which was fading fast, a strange dream of dogs and angels. My efforts were hampered somewhat by the lively chirping of cardinals, blue jays, and other birds proclaiming possession of our back yard, a symphony of avian sounds that floated through the open windows and was a pleasant distraction.

Mama and Daddy, who in their own childhood had acquired a lot of rural traits, such as rising early, had been up an hour already and were in the kitchen. Mama was at the stove frying eggs sunnyside-up in the grease of perfectly crisp bacon which lay on a paper towel to drain. Its mouth-watering smell mingled with the aroma of coffee beginning to percolate and drifted into my room, tempting me to forget the dream and to get up. A pot of grits was simmering on a back burner. Some of her homemade "heavenly grains and honey" bread waited to be toasted, then smothered with strawberry or fig preserves, the latter made by Mama with figs from our own tree.

Mama had grown up on a farm near the small town of St. George, South Carolina. She was the youngest child in a large, loving family and remained a country girl at heart who believed in big breakfasts. Although she was an enthusiastic volunteer in a number of church-related activities and was an active member of the Order of the Eastern Star, she seemed happiest as a homemaker. Naturally, one of my most vivid memories of her, years after she died, has her aproned form standing in front of the stove, a sweet smile on her face, a long-handled fork or spoon in her hand.

Daddy was sitting at the kitchen table eagerly awaiting his first cup of coffee. While waiting he sipped some freshly squeezed orange juice and read the *News and Courier*. After eating he would go to his office in the Federal Building on Meeting Street for a couple of hours.

Daddy served as District Director in Charleston for the Wage and Hour Division, U.S. Department of Labor. This is the government agency primarily responsible for enforcement of the Fair Labor Standards Act and related laws designed to protect workers against unscrupulous and careless employers. He loved his work as much as any person I have ever known. Earlier as a wage and hour investigator and later as a manager, he had received many official commendations for outstanding performance. One year he had been personally responsible for recovering over ten million dollars in back wages due hundreds of workers, many of whom lived at or near the poverty level. As a result of that feat he was summoned to the White House and, with the Secretary of Labor looking on, accepted a citation directly from the President.

He often went in to his office on Saturday but never

on Sunday. The Calvinistic heritage his grandparents brought from Scotland not only made him a conscientious worker, but also a devout keeper of the Sabbath.

Daddy's position gave him considerable prestige in the community, although civil service salaries were relatively low. That, along with his being primarily responsible for my grandmother's continuing and uninsured nursing home and medical expenses after she left Enston Homes, precluded an affluent lifestyle for us. Nevertheless, our bills were always paid on time, Ashley River Baptist Church received its tithe, and we were comfortable enough.

I was still listening to the radio (and the birds) and still trying to remember my dream when Mama called me again. This time for Daddy's sake she summoned me with mock sternness, "Andeeee, breakfast is on the table and getting cold. Please 'come and get it' right now, Son. This is the last time I'm calling you."

I knew that Daddy would be calling me next. So, to avoid what would be an unpleasant ultimatum I hopped up and into the same dirty blue jeans and tee shirt I had taken off and dropped on the bedroom floor Friday night. Then I dashed to the bathroom, splashed some water in my face, and was in the kitchen in less than thirty seconds. Almost as soon as I'd taken my usual place at the table, we heard someone knocking at the door.

Sometime during the previous night, my dog, Skibo, and a neighbor's dog, Ranger, (both half-Pekingese and half something else) had raided the neighbor's chicken pen. These otherwise lovable pets had become outlaws by digging under a fence and killing ten of Mr. Hancock's hens and two roosters before the ruckus woke him. It was Mr. Hancock who had knocked at our backdoor and who now waited there with the bad news.

Daddy answered Mr. Hancock's knock and warmly asked him to come in. With the hospitality typical of our close neighborhood, Daddy invited him to sit and have some breakfast with us. (In those days, in almost any Southern community, to be a neighbor was to be a friend.) Mr. Hancock politely declined, apologized for

interrupting our meal, and explained why he had come.

Mr. Hancock said he was taking Ranger, who he had owned as long as I had owned Skibo and who was from the same litter, to the dog pound for disposal. “Jim, I just can't put up with that kind of aggravation anymore. I'm too old,” he explained. He declined Daddy's offer to compensate him for Skibo's role in the massacre, saying, “That's right decent of you to offer, Jim, but I can't take nothing from you; I'm sure Ranger was the leader of the pack and Andy's dog was just dumb enough to follow 'im.” Nevertheless, he went on to remind Daddy and Mama of what everyone in the South knew: “Jim, Annie, it's sad but it's true: once a dog has tasted chicken blood, it's going to be a menace forever after. There's nothing in this world you can do to change 'em.”

His reminder, of course, conveyed an expectation few adults in our suburban Charleston community would consider unreasonable: Skibo should go to the pound too. Probably I turned pale at that point and my heart skipped a beat, but I knew better than to voice a protest in the presence of Mr. Hancock—it might reflect negatively on the man who was rearing me, and such an impertinence would not help Skibo's case.

Daddy's sense of duty and dedication to neighborhood harmony compelled him to assure Mr. Hancock that Skibo would be gone by sundown. “I just feel terrible about this, Earl, but I can promise you it won't happen again. Your surviving chickens ought to be able to sleep in peace tonight and lay some eggs for you in the morning.”

When Mr. Hancock left, Daddy looked first at Mama, then at me. His expression was grave as he said, “Andy, we all love Skibo, but you know as well as I what must be done. I'm sorry, Son. I'm really sorry.”

“Yes sir,” I acknowledged respectfully but somberly enough to preclude any suggestion of agreement to a death sentence for my dog which I felt was unwarranted. Surely, it being Skibo's first such offense, a measure of mercy was in order!

I think Daddy sensed my disagreement as well as my anguish, and was relieved that he could leave the scene of his judgement.

"I've got to go to the office now and get my monthly report off to Atlanta, Annie," he said to Mama. "Regional office'll be upset if it's not on their desk next week. Would you call Top and explain what's happened. I know he planned to go hunting this morning; so, he might just take Skibo to the woods with him."

Mama used her apron to wipe away the tears that the prospect of such a drastic remedy caused to course down her cheeks. She said, "Oh, Jim, there must be some way to avoid that." But she knew there was no feasible alternative and added sadly, "I'll call him."

I put some dry dog food mixed with grits left over from breakfast into Skibo's dish. While he ate, I picked off a couple of ticks and squashed them, then stroked him until my uncle drove up a half-hour later.

Of course, Skibo was hungry. Unless he was sick or in what was sometimes a week-long pursuit of a bitch in heat, he was ready to eat every morning and ready to eat again every evening. But I did not think that he and Ranger had been driven by hunger to slaughter the chickens; the dogs had killed them simply for what they must have sensed was the sport of it—in the same spirit, I suppose, as human hunters have sometimes killed elephants or eagles or other living creatures.

(Once I, too, had killed a redbird with my new BB gun. It was perched on the lower limb of a camphor tree in our front yard—and ironically, as I would learn later in high school biology, the camphor is known for its medicinal, health-enhancing, life-giving qualities. I pointed the gun and pulled the trigger. I do not know what I expected to happen, but I was not prepared to see that regal redbird fall from the tree. Dropping the gun, I ran to where the bird had fallen under an azalea bush ablaze with red blossoms. With cupped hands I raised my victim as if to comfort it, to return it to its perch, to undo what I had done. Its eyes were still open. We looked at each other in disbelief. A drop of blood no less resplendent than its feathers formed at the corner of its beak. Then, with a convulsive shiver it was free, delivered from an imperfect world of premature death at the hands of thoughtless

boys with BB guns. I wept. For days afterward I was weighted with remorse.

Subsequently, over the years in an effort to expiate my lingering guilt, I would spend hundreds of dollars on wild bird seed and feeders. I would join the Audubon Society, the Sierra Club, the South Carolina Coastal Conservation League. Psychologically, if not theologically, slaying the redbird was my original sin.)

Uncle Top was retired from the Marine Corps. He had reached the rank of "top" sergeant, hence the name by which everyone knew him. He was Mama's oldest brother and was fond enough of her to cause him always to be nice to me; however, much of his career had been spent at Parris Island as a drill instructor and often he was quite gruff or, in Daddy's opinion, a very mean man.

Of course, Daddy was not the most mellow man around town either. While I would never describe him as mean, the fact is he was more strict with me than he needed to be. Perhaps this was due to his Calvinistic conditioning; perhaps he was trying to preclude my falling from God's grace.

Uncle Top had been at Pearl Harbor when the "yellow Jap bastards," as he typically referred to them, attacked. He like to tell stories of how he had killed enemy soldiers during the war and how he had sometimes pried out their gold teeth with a bayonet. Such stories were balanced by others about Japanese atrocities and fellow Marines who had been killed, like John Zivkovic from Pittsburgh and Allan Moseley from near San Antonio.

"Ziv was the finest Yankee I ever met. Loved the Corps, loved his country and his family, and loved baseball. Planned to pitch for the Pirates after the war," Uncle Top recalled of his best buddy, who had died in his arms on Iwo Jima.

About his next best buddy, who was incinerated by a Japanese booby trap on Okinawa just three months before the atomic bomb hit Hiroshima, my uncle said: "Alamo couldn't wait to get back to his family's ranch and his high school sweetheart. Told me I'd always be welcome there. Said his girl would fix me up with a Texas heartbreaker and I'd never want to leave the Lone Star

State.

"On Okinawa, on that last day of his life, he said he was feeling lucky, that he'd be a 'Texas Ranger' for the day and volunteered to be 'point man' for our squad. His volunteering spared one of the others, probably me—it should have been my turn to be 'point.' You ask how I feel about the atomic bomb? The only thing I regret is they didn't drop the goddamned thing three months sooner."

That that remark expressed Uncle Top's true feelings was shown by naming his yacht, on which he enjoyed many days and nights of his retirement, the *Enola Gay*. This was his personal tribute to the B-29 Superfortress which dropped the bomb on Hiroshima on the morning of August 6, 1945 (a month before I entered the first grade at St. Andrew's Elementary School full of innocent patriotism and naively romantic notions about war).

"Alamo was a tough Marine, but he was also one of the gentlest, a helluva nice guy. Back at the ranch he could ride a bucking bull till the animal dropped, but he couldn't bear to stick a sizzlin' branding iron to his cattle. The hired hands always had to do it."

Because I had been weaned on World War II, my uncle was a kind of hero to me. I was particularly proud to be seen with him when he wore his uniform. I even emulated some of his mannerisms and vocabulary.

(After starting school I would be puzzled when my teachers corrected me for using the slang term for "Japanese." To myself I said, "Wasn't 'Jap' the word Uncle Top and everybody had used during the war?" Obviously, I had been much too young to enlist and could only participate vicariously, continuing to do so long after the war had ended. Standing at a toilet to pee, for example, whenever I would see someone's discarded cigarette butt floating in the bowl, I would pretend it was a Japanese battleship, the tiny shreds of tobacco its crew. As I strafed the ship, I relished watching it roll over, its hull split along the seams, and the enemy sailors spill into the boiling sea. I was too patriotic, too immature, to realize those shreds of weed represented fellow human beings with mothers and fathers, sisters and brothers, spouses, sons and daughters, all of whom grieved over

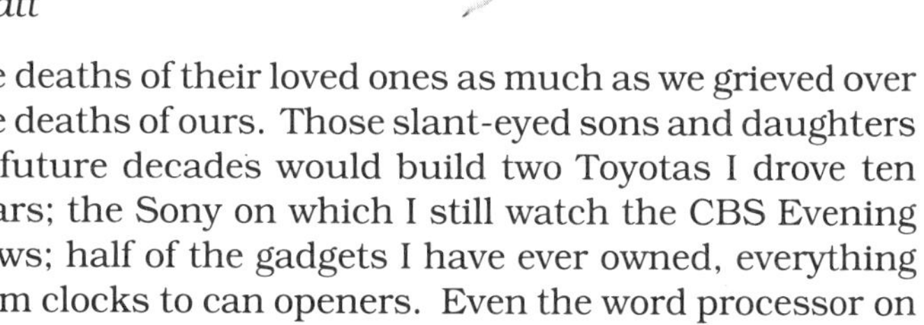

the deaths of their loved ones as much as we grieved over the deaths of ours. Those slant-eyed sons and daughters in future decades would build two Toyotas I drove ten years; the Sony on which I still watch the CBS Evening News; half of the gadgets I have ever owned, everything from clocks to can openers. Even the word processor on which I would compose my poems celebrating children, familial love, world peace—was a dependable Tandy from defeated but indefatigable Japan.)

Although I held Uncle Top in high esteem, I did not doubt his ability to execute my dog as a community service. With a stern face and military bearing he started his car and headed off on his mission. But before he was out of sight, I set off on my own mission, running to my room and kneeling at my bed.

It was a crucial moment and praying was the only thing I could do to try to save my dog's life. Uncle Top had put Skibo on the back seat of his big black Buick, a four-hole model which reminded me of the car right behind the hearse in a funeral. I could imagine one of his guns in the Buick's trunk, perhaps his new double-barreled shotgun that was decorated with engravings of game, engravings that with just a little stretch of the imagination could be seen as quasi-voodooistic.

As my heart pounded, the whispered words poured from my lips: "Please, dear Jesus, don't let Skibo be killed. He's a good dog. He didn't know killing chickens would get him into trouble. That's just the way dogs are; that's the way Your Da—Your Father, God Almighty, made them! So, spare him, Lord Jesus, and I'll do anything You want me to. I'll stop looking at those pictures of naked women in Bubba's magazines. I'll be really good and start staying for the preaching service after Sunday School with Mama and Daddy—at least every other Sunday starting tomorrow. I'll never shoot at any living thing with my BB gun again— except maybe a rattlesnake, which I don't think You'd mind because one tempted Adam and Eve in the Garden of Eden and got them to disobey the Ten Commandments and also, my daddy says, even got them to engage in *The Mating Act*! Lord, You know I haven't broken many of the

Commandments—and truly, truly, I've *never* engaged in The Mating Act.

"Anyhow, I'll do anything if You'll just let Skibo come back with Uncle Top. I promise to keep him out of trouble. Please, dear Jesus, as I ask this great favor in Your holy name. Amen."

While I never pondered the nature of prayer in childhood, I am sure I never doubted its power, its efficacy. This was one of the benefits of a Baptist boyhood. Praying was like calling someone on the rotary-dial telephone in our hallway. Throughout childhood I was blessed with good connections. It seemed Jesus was always home and always answered at the first or second ring. Most likely, inasmuch as many others with an infinite variety of praises and petitions were trying to get through to Him at the same time, He had "call-waiting" service long before it became generally available. After praying, there was no doubt that Jesus had heard my plea, had grasped the urgency of the situation, and would not let Skibo die.

In a shorter time than it seemed, Uncle Top returned. He pulled off the road and parked beside our mailbox. The car door opened. Skibo darted out and ran to me, then ran in circles around me, wagging his tail furiously, jumping, and yelping with delight. It had become an endearing ritual he always went through whenever we were reunited even after brief separations. I was relieved, full of joy, and grateful for what I felt was divine kindness; I knew, however, that things could not be the way they had been before the chickens were killed.

Mama came out to the porch drying her hands on her apron. She had a surprised look on her face as she pushed a wisp of pretty blonde hair from her forehead. Seeing his favorite sibling, Uncle Top smiled and began to explain. "Well, Annie," he said, "I took Andy's dog down Savage Road into the woods. I stopped and let him get out. Swampy down there—mosquitoes were thick. He just sat there on the side of the road while I took my double-barreled shotgun from the trunk. I loaded the gun and he still just sat there on his haunches looking up at me. I raised the gun to my shoulder and he didn't

flinch. It was like he'd resigned himself to his fate. He was as brave as a Marine.

"Just then the reddest bird I think I've ever seen zoomed in and perched on a branch almost directly over the dog's head. And that darn bird spread its wings and started to sing! Reminded me of an angel somehow—so pretty and sounded so sweet it was downright distracting. But I had a job to do and squeezed the trigger. It just clicked. Misfire. That happens once in a while. So, I squeezed the other trigger—and 'click' again. I removed those shells from the gun and got two more from a brand-new box. Put them in, closed the chamber, raised the gun to my shoulder again. The dog hadn't moved an inch, just wagged his tail a little. I pulled the right trigger, half-expecting by then the 'click' I got. Then the left trigger. When that shell misfired too, I said to myself, 'Jesus Christ! Somebody's prayed for this dog—I'm going to take it home to Tommy.'"

And I swear that is what Uncle Top said happened. Fortunately, their house was just a few miles away and right across Savannah Highway from our church, so I was able to play with my cousin Tommy and Skibo often. They had a large, fenced-in yard, and no chickens were anywhere near. Skibo had a good life there and eventually died of old age.

* * *

Years later at the University of South Carolina, I majored in English, assuming it would help me to refine my own prose and poetry, and that it might be useful preparation for law school, about which I vacillated from week to week. As importantly, in terms of helping me define my values, I minored in philosophy and religion. One day during my senior year, the shotgun incident came to mind as I reread the Gospel story about feeding the multitude with only five loaves of bread and two fish. I was preparing a term paper on miracles and wondering if what happened on that grassy hillside overlooking the Sea of Galilee had been a phenomenon which defied God's own natural laws—or whether it had been, more

beautifully, a miracle of the spirit.

In comparing the story's details as they are related in each of the four Gospels, I was especially intrigued by John's account. Only he mentions Andrew, my ancient namesake, telling Jesus, "There is a lad here, who hath five barley loaves and two small fishes; but what are they among so many?" Leave it to John, I thought, an apostle who emphasized love more than law, to give a credit to a nameless little boy whose humble gesture of generosity shamed his elders into breaking out the food hidden under their robes and sharing with those who had nothing to eat, a sharing epitomizing the Golden Rule. That the "haves" had brought more than they needed for themselves seems evidenced by the twelve full baskets of leftovers . . . .

At length I thought about the "miracle" on Savage Road. Admittedly, although it added a nice touch to Uncle Top's story, I had always been a bit skeptical about the redbird alighting over Skibo. For the first time, however, I wondered whether my uncle's shotgun had really misfired or if it were simply an overpowering image of boy and dog in his mind, an image from his own childhood or of his own son, perhaps, which represented the answer to my prayer. It also occurred to me that there really had been a redbird which seemed like an angel telling him not to pull the trigger and that he had simply obeyed his strange intuition. In any case, I am sure the misfiring shotgun version of the story would have been easier for any Marine sergeant to tell. For me, all the possibilities are equally miraculous.

Boys and Bridges

In the fall of the year Bubba and I were in the eighth grade at St. Andrew's Junior High School, we began drifting apart. We had no classes together and rarely saw each other after school. When we happened to meet by chance and chat even briefly, I was aware of a growing streak of rebellion in him. On one of those occasions he expressed admiration for actor James Dean and talked enthusiastically about Dean's character role in the popular film *Rebel Without a Cause.* The encounter left me with a foreboding of Bubba somehow seeking to emulate that star-crossed character.

By then this still dear friend, who until shortly before had also been my almost constant companion, was hanging out with a rough group of older boys whom my parents had cautioned me to avoid. Bubba was apparently even affecting their crude language in order to be accepted by that group. I was taken aback by it as well as by a strong odor of cigarette smoke about him. We had been best friends all through childhood, and this apparent change in his personality which coincided with our reaching puberty was unsettling.

"*Rebel* is one helluva flick, Andy. Fuckin' fine. Jòe Morgan took a bunch of us to see it at the Magnolia Drive-In Saturday night. Joe drove that sporty new Mercury of his—sharpest car in town, by the way—he drove in at the box office; the rest of us sneaked in across the field. Anyhow, you've got to see it, man," he urged me.

"I've heard a lot about it, Bubba, and want to go. But why did y'all sneak into the Magnolia? That's like stealing, isn't it? Don't you get an allowance anymore?"

"For Christ's sake, Andy, get off my case. When are you going to grow out of your 'John the Baptist' mode and

start having some fun? It may've been cute when we were little kids, but we're *big boys* now. Sneaking in doesn't have anything to do with money; it's *fun* to sneak in. It's just plain damn fun!"

"If Mr. Sanders catches your butts doing that, I'll bet you won't think it's so much fun," I warned of the stern manager, who went to our church and was generally considered to be a pretty nice fellow.

"Yeah, well, the turd'll have to catch us first. Meanwhile, you'll be happy to know we're planning to sneak in to hear 'Elvis the Pelvis' at College Park next week. Damn tickets cost as much as a couple of cartons of Camels. Want to come?"

In April our principal caught Bubba smoking in the restroom and suspended him for three days. Despite his suspension and growing tendency to finesse his schoolwork, Bubba bordered on being brilliant and had the ability to absorb enough information even while daydreaming in class to pass his exams. His grades slipped a bit but remained well above average. Both of us looked forward to receiving our junior high school diplomas the first Friday night in June.

For post-commencement celebration, Bubba and a bunch of his new buddies had plans to pile into Joe Morgan's Mercury with a case of beer and go cruising. Joe's car, a two-door hardtop, was nicely outfitted for this activity: chrome-plated dual exhausts, white sidewalls, fender skirts, rear-mounted radio antennas, and an "oo-guh" horn. The car also had a unique paint job, which was really quite pretty and not nearly as shocking as it might sound. Joe described it as "pussy wagon pink 'n purple." More precisely, the "pink" was fuchsia. His car was his pride and joy.

Joseph Anthony Morgan was a senior at Murray Vocational School and had studied auto mechanics there since the ninth grade. He worked part time at Mark's Garage and was considered to be a good worker. His father, a soldier, was killed in the Normandy landings, one of those in the first wave of invaders who died in the water at Omaha Beach.

To add misfortune to misfortune, too soon after

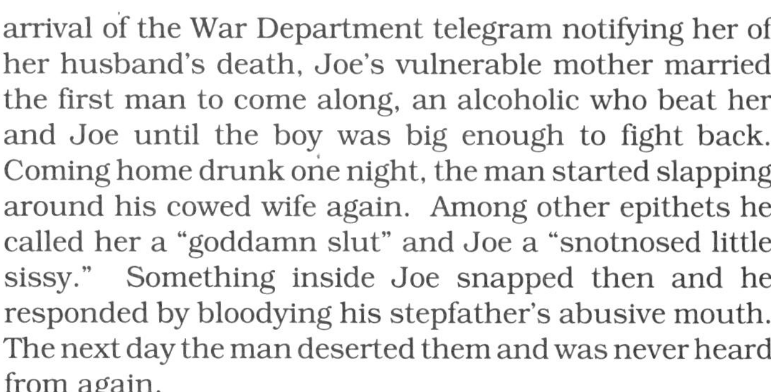

arrival of the War Department telegram notifying her of her husband's death, Joe's vulnerable mother married the first man to come along, an alcoholic who beat her and Joe until the boy was big enough to fight back. Coming home drunk one night, the man started slapping around his cowed wife again. Among other epithets he called her a "goddamn slut" and Joe a "snotnosed little sissy." Something inside Joe snapped then and he responded by bloodying his stepfather's abusive mouth. The next day the man deserted them and was never heard from again.

Throughout a traumatic childhood, Joe longed to be an adult. Later, due to a rumor that he had "done it," Joe would not only be envied, but also esteemed by many of the other boys in the community. For an eighteen-year-old, he had quite a following of loyal friends and deferential fans.

In fact, it was his father's death that eventually made possible Joe's new Mercury. Sgt. Morgan had purchased a small insurance policy on himself right before his unit was shipped to England in preparation for D-Day. The policy named his son as beneficiary. An amendment to it provided that any benefits otherwise payable would be held in trust, together with accumulating interest, until Joe's eighteenth birthday. The father's intent was that, in the event of his death, his son would have some funds for college. Instead, Joe opted to give himself the most fantastic birthday present of his life, one which promised to make up for a lot of losses.

* * *

Right before the ceremony, as the candidates for graduation waited to process into the auditorium, Bubba invited me to join his group afterwards: "Come on, Andy. We haven't had any fun together this whole damned school year. A little merrymaking's in order. We're just going to cruise over to Folly and maybe pick up some chicks." Whispering into my ear, he added, "And maybe get some pussy!" Then, as my face reddened, he playfully punched my arm and, displaying his unique grin, a grin as mischievous as it was engaging, he said, "Just some good, clean, all-American fun, you know?"

And I had to say, "Thanks, Bubba, but there's no use even asking my parents. I know they wouldn't let me go. Just have some extra fun for me, will you?"

Afterwards, Joe and the others were waiting for Bubba in the school parking lot. The others included Ben and Jerry West, who were cousins, and Nick Milano. With a showy squeal of the tires, they pulled out onto Wappoo Road in the direction of Dupont's Crossing. Bubba pleaded, "Hey, Joe, go easy on the rubber—at least until we're away from the damn school and my old man. He'd shit a squash if he'd seen that!"

"Dupont's Crossing" actually designated a pair of diagonal intersections. One was where the Seaboard Railroad tracks crossed Wappoo Road; the other, about forty or fifty yards away, was where the same tracks crossed U.S. 17, better known on the west side of Charleston as Savannah Highway. As the Mercury approached the Wappoo Road crossing, the semaphore was on to warn that a train was coming. Joe slowed to stop, but Ben egged him on: "We'll be here all night if we have to wait for a friggin' freight train a mile long. Goose it over, man!"

The Mercury accelerated across the tracks with just seconds to spare and immediately pulled into Whaley's Gulf Station on the triangular corner lot bordered by the railroad tracks, Wappoo Road, and Savannah Highway. No one in the car paid any attention to the short six-unit passenger train as it clattered past with a sharp blast from its horn.

Joe told Sonny Grant, the usually jovial attendant who approached the car to pump their gas, "Fill 'er up with high-test, Sonny. We got some cruisin' to do tonight, man."

Sonny said somberly, "You white boys better be more careful. I saw that train almost get you," and he proceeded to pump the gas.

Joe had a standard cocky reply for such occasions: "Counts as a miss, don't it? Besides, if I were to die, the Devil wouldn't know what to do with me." Everybody laughed.

As a matter of course, Sonny checked the car's oil and cleaned its windshield. Joe handed Sonny a five dollar bill and received some change. With a full tank of gas under a full case of beer, the group turned east on Savannah Highway and headed for Folly Beach, thirteen miles away. About a mile down the two-lane highway and near the Magnolia Drive-In Theatre, a police car came up behind the Mercury and sounded its siren. Joe pulled over saying, "Shit. Everybody, hide your cans and keep cool. I'll handle this."

The police officer walked up to the driver's window and looked everyone over with his flashlight. "You young fellows seem to be in a awfully big hurry." Then looking again at Bubba he added, "And aren't you Mr. Billy Brinson's boy?"

"Yes sir."

"Well, most of us on the force think your dad's going to be our next circuit judge. Hope he'll be. Fine man. You think he'd be pleased to know y'all were out here weaving in and out of traffic like that?"

Bubba had recognized his interrogator as Cpl. Larry Long, a "good old boy" he knew his father had successfully defended once in a paternity suit. He also realized the value of courtesy in a situation like this: "You're right, Officer Long, and we're sorry. You see, sir, we just had graduation at St. Andrew's Junior High tonight. I got my diploma and—well, we were all just going over to the beach to celebrate. We three on the back seat were making a lot of noise and trying to distract the driver. It's more our fault than his, sir."

Officer Long, impressed by Bubba's chivalrous attitude (as well as wishing, perhaps, to earn a few Brownie points with a prospective judge), said, "I can understand that—everybody likes to celebrate and gets carried away once in a while." Then in a sterner voice he spoke to Joe: "Even so, the way you were driving since back there at Dupont's Crossing, y'all'll be dead before you can celebrate anything. I'm going to let you go without a ticket this time. But I warn you, if you get stopped again, you'll be in trouble. Now you boys ought

to be able to drive safely and have fun at the same time. Isn't that what being young's all about? How about it, Mr. Morgan?"

"Thank you, sir. I'll do better. That's a promise," Joe lied.

The Mercury bore right on Stocker Drive, an affluent avenue of large brick and stone homes curving through the heart of Windermere, and only slowed for the stop sign at Folly Road. This is the road that would take the group to the edge of the continent ten miles south, the edge where concrete and asphalt end and close to the very edge where sand meets sea.

About a mile farther along, they approached Wappoo Cut Creek and the first of many bridges they would have to cross before reaching their ultimate destination. But, as their luck would have it that fateful night, before the group could get across this first one, the bridge's warning lights started blinking.

Off to the right in the Atlantic Intracoastal Waterway, a sleek sailboat approached the center of the bridge under auxiliary power. The boat's sails were furled and its stern bore the prophetic name "Saint Christopher."

If the boat's name had been discernible to him, Bubba might have instinctively squeezed the St. Christopher medal he wore on a silver chain around his neck and kept discreetly under his shirt. The medal was not only a memento of his many summer sessions at Camp St. Christopher, an Episcopal Church camp and conference facility on nearby Seabrook Island, but also a talisman. It was a talisman he continued to wear even though he rarely thought of the third century saint whose image it bore.

Nevertheless, if anyone were interested enough to ask him, Bubba could discuss intelligently the lovely legend of St. Christopher. The legend involves Christopher compassionately carrying a child across a river, a child whose weight upon Christopher's shoulders became almost unbearable, and his discovery then that he was carrying Jesus, who carried in His own hands the whole world.

As the patron saint of travelers, Christopher was a

good man to carry along wherever one was going, be it to some place near like one's local "Folly Beach" or to the ends of the earth. Bubba never left home without him.

"Probably some rich damn Yankees on their way back from fuckin' Florida. They should have to wait for us when they're in Rebel territory," Ben said from the shotgun seat.

Joe took Ben's comment as a challenge. The Mercury rushed past the blinking red signals. The group's luck with lights—or perhaps better said, the group's luck in disregarding lights intended to save their lives—held for a second time that night.

They fooled around Folly Beach for a while, then left for the proverbial greener pastures, in this case the Isle of Palms. You might reasonably guess one of them said something like, "No decent chicks here anyhow. Let's check out the Beach Comber on the Isle. Should be some shaggin' there tonight." Of course, in those days there were likely to be as many pretty girls at the Folly Beach pavilion as at the Beach Comber or anywhere else. It is also likely that it was the hunters who were not "decent" enough to entice the intended prey.

Recrossing the Wappoo Cut bridge, Jerry West said from the back seat, "Damn, Joe, no red lights to run this time? That's a crying shame."

As if that were his cue, Nick Milano, who fancied himself to be Charleston's answer to Frank Sinatra, began singing the popular song "Ain't That a Shame." Joe interrupted him, "I guess the word's got out: Joe Morgan and his gang don't stop for no red lights or nothin'." And there was laughter again.

But a person can hardly get from one place to any other place in the Charleston area without crossing a bridge. In that sense Charleston may be much like Venice—and five more stood between these young cruisers, who were more brash than bold, and the shagging sweeties of their fantasies: the suntanned teenaged girls they imagined to be awaiting them with open arms and damp panties on the Isle of Palms.

In a world where almost everything is genderized, (that is, categorized as either male or female) everything

from electrical fixtures to biological organisms, and including ships, moons, countries, churches, even hurricanes, it should not be considered sexist to note bridges have an unmistakable quality of femininity: they receive and bear the weight of whatever enters or rolls over them. Longer bridges are often graceful works of engineering art, sometimes suggestive of a prima donna; shorter bridges are almost always cute and appear fecund. Who among us has never experienced a subtle sense of satisfaction, release, or even exhilaration at the end of traversing a long, slender bridge?

The first of these five bridges crossed the Ashley River as gracefully as any American bridge crosses any river. Its architecture, even it not Venetian, had an Old World quality. Unfortunately, its charm would be compromised later by the construction of a twin span parallel to it. But the twin, if anything, was fraternal, not identical.

In the river to the right, small waves rippled the reflections of lights on the masts of ships berthed at the Naval Minecraft Base. Topside a few sailors on each ship stood watch in the marsh-scented night. Below deck others from states as far flung as Mississippi and Minnesota lay in their bunks to read paperbacks, write letters to wives and sweethearts, or sleep. Some crewmembers were still out on liberty, enjoying the "beer joints and broads" for which Market Street was noted (before it was placed off-limits to military personnel and long before it evolved into a street of chic shops, luxury hotels, and trendy restaurants).

Next in line of the five was the Grace Memorial Bridge, better known to locals by the name of the Cooper River it still crosses at a maximum height of about 150 feet. Two spans, joined at Drum Island, total two miles in length. When completed in 1929, it was one of the longest cantilever bridges in the world. If no longer one of the highest, it remains among the most breathtaking. For many it is as romantic as San Francisco's Golden Gate; for many others it inspires as much parochial pride as the Brooklyn Bridge.

Coming down the very steep span into Mount Pleasant, the Mercury was moving much faster than the speed limit. The county policeman who gave chase at the bottom of the bridge estimated the car to be traveling at close to seventy miles per hour. It was about eleven o'clock and little traffic was on the highway as Joe saw the flashing red light in his rearview mirror and decided to try to lose his pursuer in the maze of short streets on Sullivan's Island. "I'll lose that cocksucker," he boasted to his crew, all of whom had drunk too much beer to be able to reason with him.

The pursued and pursuer raced along Coleman Boulevard in the center of the sleeping community. Their speed soon exceeded eighty miles per hour.

The third of the five bridges lies across Shem Creek. This bridge is level and short. At eighty miles an hour, a car crosses it in less than two seconds. Along both sides of the creek were popular seafood restaurants, one of which was a favorite of the Brinsons. There was also an ice cream shop where Ben and Jerry had worked part time until the owner discovered the two cousins were giving away to friends as much ice cream as they sold.

In the tidal creek itself, which connected with the harbor and in turn widened into the Atlantic Ocean, were docked a fleet of shrimp boats. These sturdy boats, perhaps because they were ceremoniously blessed every spring by a local priest, kept the nearby restaurants well supplied with succulent shrimp as well as fresh flounder, dolphin, and other fish. On board the boats, their nets hung from booms to dry. Seagulls perched on the nets to sleep and to await their share of the next day's catch.

The Mercury passed Moultrie High School, rounded a curve on two squealing tires, then crossed a long causeway through marsh leading to the Ben Sawyer Bridge, fourth of the five. On the other side of this bridge awaited the presumed sanctuary of Sullivan's Island where they planned to lose their pursuer before continuing their odyssey. Sullivan's Island, as the site of a significant Revolutionary War victory for a group challenging the establishment, and as the setting for one of Edgar Allan Poe's best-known stories, *The Gold Bug*, would be perfect for that phase of the adventure.

The police officer chased the boys over the causeway

but began to slow when he saw what was happening ahead. It was never known for sure whether or not Joe saw the bridge's signal arms come down across the roadway and its somewhat unusual swing span begin to rotate. Perhaps he did see the bridge was opening but was determined to make good his boast. Perhaps he was going too fast to stop even if he had wanted. In any case, the pink and purple Mercury left no skid marks.

Splintering the wooden signal arm, the car reached the end of the roadway instantly and was airborne for several seconds, a purgatorial period of time which must have seemed more like minutes or hours to the terrified occupants. The car hit and ricocheted from the outside of the span's steel supports, losing a door, fender, hubcaps, and other parts in the process. It then spun completely around with what could have been a final sound from its "oo-guh" horn and snapped in half the wooden mast of a sailboat for which the bridge had opened before splashing into the Intracoastal Waterway.

Slamming on his brakes, the police officer was able to stop at the very edge of the briny abyss. The red light atop his cruiser continued to flash as he leaped out and looked over.

The bridge tender was alert. He took note of the police's presence and immediately called the nearby Coast Guard station. He ascertained that the mastless sailboat, which happened to be named "Saint Christopher" and was on its way home to Newport, Rhode Island, was out of the way of the span and not sinking. Then he brought the swing span around to the closed position, leaving the bridge's warning lights flashing. This, he thought, would slow traffic and facilitate rescue efforts.

A few passersby who stopped to help had flashlights, but their narrow beams revealed only an oil slick and bits of debris on the water's surface. Beneath that dark surface was a carload of fun-loving boys. Already these boys were dead or dying in the briny water which had filled their noses and ears, their mouths and throats, their lungs and stomachs.

Several other police officers arrived and tried to keep

traffic moving, tried to keep the way clear for emergency vehicles. Naturally, their efforts were hampered by the concerned and the curious who virtually ignored the barked orders: "Keep moving! Don't stop. Keep moving or you'll be arrested. Please keep moving."

As minutes passed without anybody rising to the surface, the mood of the onlookers and rescuers became somber. Soon the Coast Guard was at the scene with searchlights and a diver located the sunken car. The diver began bringing up bodies. It was too late for resuscitation but the rescuers tried anyway. A woman among the onlookers became hysterical. She was sobbing, "That one looks like my boy. O God, please make him breath," as she was led away by her husband. (This couple had never seen these dead boys before, although they had lost one of their own sons in another automobile accident on the same highway a year earlier, and that son's older brother had been killed in the Korean War.)

In the edge of the marsh a hundred yards from the bridge, the sole survivor lay dazed. He was still clinging to a piece of the sailboat mast he instinctively grabbed when thrown from the car on its way into the water. The mast had broken off so that it looked like a cross, and this battered boy appeared to have been crucified on it. Although his clothes were torn and his shoes were missing, a silver chain and medal were still intact around his neck. A piece of seaweed or marsh grass was wrapped around his bruised head like a crown of thorns. He was covered with pluff mud, which acted as the salve of his salvation in stemming the flow of blood from numerous cuts. Several Coast Guardsmen waded into the marsh with a stretcher and brought Bubba back to a waiting ambulance.

* * *

The fifth of the five bridges, one which would not have the honor of bearing the masculine weight of the Mercury that night, crosses Breach Inlet. The inlet itself is a treacherous place for swimming and has claimed a hundred of the unwary who insist on risking it, drowning

after drowning.

On the other side of the inlet lies the Isle of Palms. Like Folly and Sullivan's Islands, it is one of the dozens of typically long, narrow barrier islands which help to insulate the inland of the Lowcountry from periodic agitations of the Atlantic. The Isle of Palms was best known for its beautiful strand, usually gentle surf, and, of course, the Beach Comber.

At the Beach Comber a big crowd of young people from every corner of Charleston County was gathered and having fun. They filled the interior of the establishment and spilled onto an open deck facing the ocean. Ironically, there were noticeably more girls than guys. There were cheerleader types, Ashley Hall types, girl-next-door types, not one of whom was undesirable. Their names ranged alphabetically from "Angela," "Betty," and "Caroline" to "Yolanda" and "Zelda."

The ambiance was like that of an open party. To the rhythmic music of the Geechees, a popular local band, these carefree Carolinians alternately slow danced and shagged the summer night away. Had Joe's gang arrived, it is statistically possible one of them may have scored; it is probable they all would have had *fun.*

Missy & Me

The next day was Saturday. It was also the first day of summer vacation. Having received on the previous evening the St. Andrew's Junior High School diploma for which I had striven two difficult years, I had decided I deserved a rest and would sleep late that morning. (Unlike Bubba, I had to work hard for my A's and B's.) Moreover, I had gone to bed feeling disappointed about not getting to go out with Bubba's group after the graduation ceremony. Or, more accurately, I may have been feeling disappointed with myself for not at least asking my parents for permission to go. Who knows? A respectful request might have caught them at a weak moment, or they even may have been inclined to be indulgent on such a happy, milestone occasion for me. Subconsciously, I may have felt sleeping late would be an antidote for my disappointment.

I awoke about my usual time, however, with thoughts like "No school today!" and "Free to do as I please until after Labor Day!" overcoming any lingering sense of loss about the missed opportunity. Then, still lying in bed as was my custom, I tried to remember the details of what seemed like a nightlong bad dream. The vivid images of the dream were already fading, although I could remember Bubba and I being out in his father's small sailboat, something which in reality we had not done together since July or August of the previous summer. We must have been some distance offshore because we had lost sight of land. Then a severe squall developed, overtaking us very quickly and even before we could lower the sail. The boat's mast snapped and knocked Bubba overboard. Leaning over the side of the boat, I desperately tried to catch one of his frantically flailing arms, but he remained frustratingly just beyond my reach. It seemed strange I would dream something like that—was there a message, I wondered. Was Bubba in some kind of danger?

Daddy happened to be listening to an early morning newscast on the radio when he heard what had happened on the Ben Sawyer Bridge the night before. He hurried into my room and shook my shoulder, saying, "Andy. Andy, wake up."

Startled, I turned toward him and said, "I'm awake, Daddy."

"Bubba Brinson's been in a terrible accident and is in the hospital. News report didn't say which one, and the Brinsons' phone doesn't answer. But we can call around and find out where he is. It's terrible. Some other boys drowned."

I jumped up asking, "Accident? What happened? How badly is Bubba hurt, Daddy? And who drowned?"

"I'll tell you what details I know when you get some clothes on—I'm going to start calling the hospitals."

Dressing quickly, I called, "Daddy, can we go see him when you find out where he is?" Daddy did not answer but was already talking on the phone and may not have heard me.

My concern consumed me. It also made me realize Bubba was still my best friend. Bowing my head, I remembered my dream and whispered, "Please be with Bubba, sweet Jesus; be with Bubba and bring him through this. And please bring us close together again."

At St. Francis Xavier Hospital my parents and I found Bubba heavily sedated and well bandaged. A nun who was a nurse was taking his temperature. A bottle of blood plasma hung beside his bed, a tube connecting the bottle to his body. A crucifix on the wall behind the head of the bed was a silent reminder, among other things, of the hospital staff's devotion to God and dedication to caring for the ill and injured, not only with technical competence, but also with compassion.

A grateful Mr. Brinson stepped out into the hallway with us and said, "He had multiple lacerations and lost a lot of blood. But, miraculously, there were no broken bones or internal injuries. Bubba's guardian angel must have been expecting something like this and was ready to throw him on that sailboat mast. But those other poor fellows—my heart is so heavy for their families. It's tragic." Mr. Brinson's eyes were wet.

Leaving the hospital, we saw Mrs. Brinson and Missy coming toward us across the parking lot. They were returning for a second visit with the injured prodigal son. Missy carried Bubba's radio, which they anticipated he would want as soon as his sedation wore off. While Mrs. Brinson told my parents how she feared something like this would happen, Missy walked ahead. I caught up with her, lightly touching her arm and saying softly, "Missy, I'm glad Bubba's going to be alright."

"Thanks, Andy," was all she said, but a wan smile let me know she appreciated my concern for her brother. Perhaps it conveyed something else as well. Often, shared concerns do draw people closer . . . .

Bubba was out of the hospital in a few days. I visited him at home the day after his release. Missy had gone to the library to get a book for him. Mrs. Brinson took me to his room, then left us. I had brought a gift. "Bubba, here's the new *Sports Illustrated.* You're in luck—it's the annual bathing suit issue. I was going to buy *Playboy* for you, but it was already sold out everywhere I looked."

"You lie through your teeth, Andy, but thanks anyway," he said, trying to be friendly and forcing a smile. He knew I would not risk discovery by my parents, and their wrath, by buying a magazine like *Playboy* anywhere within a hundred miles of Charleston.

Bubba seemed to be more subdued than I had ever remembered. He mourned the deaths of his companions and was silent for a while. Forcing another smile, he said, "I think I have a better appreciation now for how Jonah must have felt in the belly of that whale. The few seconds I was fully submerged in the water has made me think a lot about that story."

Then he announced, "My folks have decided I should go to boarding school in Virginia in September. They first suggested the idea to me a month or two ago. I'd hoped

it was too late to apply for admission this fall, but Uncle Middleton is on the board, so the headmaster assured him they would be pleased to find a place for me. There's nothing like being well-connected, is there?

"I'm not excited about leaving all my friends, those who are still alive anyway. Like you, of course, Andy. But I guess it's the best thing, considering the circumstances, isn't it? I can get a new start there, they say. Can't you just see me, though, at an Episcopal boarding school? Sitting in a Latin class in a coat-and-tie uniform with all those prissy, preppy little punks? I'll bet you my folks will insist I go to Sewanee after that and eventually to some goddamned seminary. They didn't name me Middleton Jackson Brinson for nothing. No sir, you can bet your ass on that."

"Everything will work out alright," I assured him. "You might end up following in your Uncle Middleton's famous footsteps—you just might be 'Bishop Bubba' someday. Meanwhile, if I know you, you'll teach those cloistered kids something about real life, life in the raw, and so forth."

"Well, I'm just not interested in being a 'Bishop Bubba,' a Buddha, or anything else that requires wearing a stiff collar or quaint costume all the time."

"Look, we'll miss you down here in the boondocks, but you'll be right across the river from Washington. So maybe you'll get to see the Senators play sometime. You'll have lots of adventures to tell your old underprivileged friends about when you're home on vacation."

"Yeah," Bubba said with a sigh, "and maybe you could even come up to Alexandria with my folks for a long weekend or something." Then after a long pause he added, "It's awkward to say this, so I'm only going to say it once. There are a lot of guys around town like those I almost drowned with. But you're different, Andy. You're really a decent fellow. Missy thinks so, too. And she's special even if she is my sister. Both of you could do a whole lot worse, you know?"

Taken aback by this apparent encouragement from a dear friend to court his sister, I just said, "I know, Bubba—that Missy's special, I mean. Don't worry, I'll

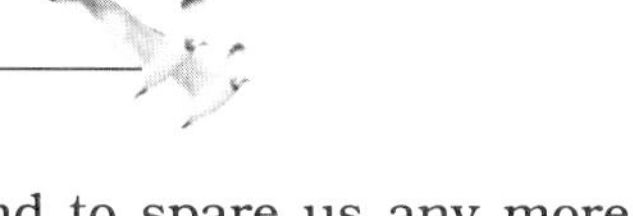

look out for her." And to spare us any more mutual embarrassment, I quickly added, "Look, I've some errands to run, but I'll see you before you leave for Virginia."

When summer ended and school resumed, Bubba was at the Episcopal School for Boys, I was in the ninth grade at St. Andrew's Parish High, and Missy was in the seventh grade of St. Andrew's Junior High. One large two-storied brick building with white columns housed grades seven through twelve, so on most days I saw Missy in the hallway or on the grounds at recess. Often there was only time enough to exchange "Hi's" or to wave. I rarely called her at home—Daddy frowned on my using the phone too much—but a rapport was slowly growing between us.

Bubba did not do well his first year in boarding school. Surprisingly, he barely passed. Perhaps his poor performance was due to the difficult adjustment of being five hundred miles from home, from family, and from friends he was not ready to leave. When he came home on Christmas vacation we talked and I sensed there was something more than distance bothering him. I wondered if he were still troubled by the accident at the bridge. I asked if he ever thought of the incident and received a pained reply.

"Yes," he admitted, "I think of it every day, Andy. Every night when I lie down to sleep, every morning when I wake up. I can see those happy-go-lucky guys running out of luck, see them sobering in the instant we crashed through the lowered signal arms, glass shattering, their silly grins turned into grimaces of horror. I can see myself flying through the air and hitting the water. I see her—there's something I—don't make me talk about it anymore, Andy. It still hurts too much."

I never brought up the subject again, although he would bring it up once more some years later.

Bubba chose to remain at boarding school the following summer for remedial work. His family went up to visit him but he did not come to Charleston at all that summer. Consequently, among other things, he missed out on the month they traditionally spent at their Sullivan's

Island beach house. His sacrifice of summer fun and tan paid off, however, and Bubba began to excel in his sophomore year. In his senior year his application to the University of the South in Sewanee, Tennessee, his Uncle Middleton's alma mater, would be promptly answered with an enthusiastic letter of acceptance.

The Brinsons had long been close friends of my parents and we were regular visitors at their beach house. It seemed odd for Bubba not to be there the summer he stayed in Virginia, but his absence allowed Missy and me to spend more time alone with each other than ever before. We swam in the surf, we played paddleball on the beach, we sat and talked on the sand dunes under the stars.

Those starlight talks were innocent, but they were invariably stimulating. Missy was bright beyond her tender years. We talked about school, movies, books, popular and classical music, religion, our aspirations for the future, and life in general, including the nature of the universe. Well, we did muse over many of its mysteries and some of its paradoxes. Often, mesmerized by the night sky's constellations, planets, occasional meteors, we touched on this. More than once Missy asked, "How can you talk about 'the expanding universe,' Andy? What's it expanding into?"

"Into the vacuum of empty space," I replied, knowing it was an inadequate answer that would raise her next question.

"And how far does that empty space extend, Mr. Andy Astronomer?"

"Up to the pearly gates of Heaven, I guess," I said facetiously.

That we never reached a definitive conclusion about what might lie on the other side of the universe's expanding boundaries was not unsatisfactory; it only made the conversations—and our being together—all the more stimulating.

Up at the beach house, our parents would be sitting on the screened porch. In rocking chairs, they faced the Atlantic Ocean for the full effect of its refreshing breeze and enjoyed some after dinner coffee and solace of

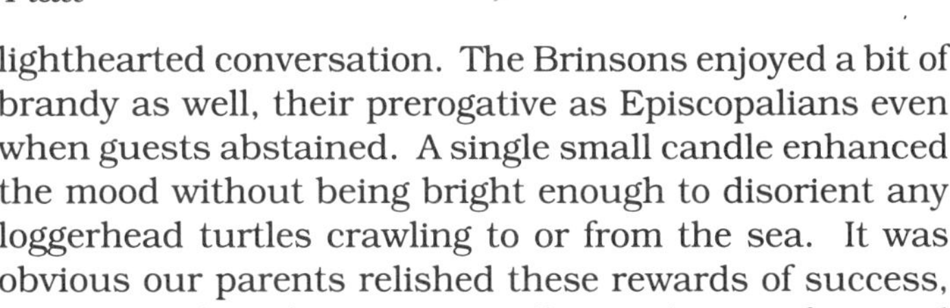

lighthearted conversation. The Brinsons enjoyed a bit of brandy as well, their prerogative as Episcopalians even when guests abstained. A single small candle enhanced the mood without being bright enough to disorient any loggerhead turtles crawling to or from the sea. It was obvious our parents relished these rewards of success, success in their domestic as well as in their professional lives.

During pauses in our own conversation out on the dunes, Missy and I could sometimes hear their laughter in the cool, seaside air. Hearing them, I would be momentarily envious of the satisfactions I imagined to await them in their respective beds. I was eager to be older. Being married to someone you love, I thought, must be like being in heaven.

I was fifteen that summer and Missy a new teenager. Something good, something deeper than just rapport seemed to be developing between us—something too tender to be risked by doing anything that might make her feel uncomfortable with me. The striptease incident two years earlier was never alluded to. Whenever we were together, I was always careful to avoid any comment or gesture that might seem suggestive. Nevertheless, she had my attention, and my fertile imagination could not be curbed.

Missy was slightly tall for her age and willowy. Her chin was dimpled. Her nose, knees, and ankles were sculpted. The freckles were less prominent now and the braces gone from nearly perfect teeth. These attributes were complemented by green eyes and long red hair, sometimes pony-tailed, sometimes framing her angelic face like a halo. She was naturally well-coordinated. The dance lessons she had taken since the second grade with the Robert Ivey Ballet gave her grace and poise as well. She was active enough to be healthy and she looked it. If any thirteen-year-old girl could be described as "beautiful," Missy fit the description. She was bright and beautiful.

Eventually, with Bubba so far away most of the time, I began to feel free to court Missy. I no longer felt bound by the taboo Southern boys honor by not dating, and

certainly not seducing, their friends' sisters.

The USC Knights

Last summer, after seeing and being moved again by the poetic film *Field of Dreams*, I became caught up with the World Series. Soon I was transfixed in front of my television (a real novelty for me), watching every game and rooting for the team I perceived to the underdog and, therefore, presumably the more *Southern* of the two. The experience prompted me to dig out some old notes on one of the most memorable lectures I ever heard as a student at the University of South Carolina. It was delivered by my sociology professor, Dr. Daniel Jones, affectionately referred to as "Dirty Dan" by his otherwise respectful, admiring students.

Dr. Jones, a U.S.C. alumnus who had earned his Ph.D. at the University of Chicago, was too concerned with matters of the mind to care much about his outward appearance. It was said that one could tell what he had had to eat for the previous six months just by looking at his variegated necktie. His office, too, was a mess. Ashtrays and wastebaskets overflowed; books, papers, scholarly journals, etc., were piled on his desk, on a couple of tables, and on the filthy rug beside his fully packed floor-to-ceiling bookcases.

Although my transcription may not be verbatim, I was adept at a simplified style of shorthand, and present the following as essentially what Dr. Jones, my brilliant, somewhat whimsical professor, had to say:

> Those who study the culture of the modern South seriously and in depth are likely to find sports have a more significant role than may have been suspected. Sports in the South are not

merely amusement. They may amuse, but they do more. One can begin to examine this thesis by considering sports in the context of something very familiar to most of us, familial relationships. In this region where such relationships are of fundamental importance to the fabric of our society, involvement either directly or indirectly with team sports often provides the participants with surrogate families, supplemental families, or both.

Contact sports, which in the South means primarily football, have an additional dimension. Each season, each game gives all the participants, not only the players on the field, but also supporters on the sidelines, in the stands, and in front of television screens, another chance to exact revenge or to redeem themselves for the loss of the most important contest in our corporate history, the Civil War. Obviously, such motivations tend to be subliminal and, therefore, hard to substantiate; on the other hand, they are difficult to disprove. In any case, a century after it was fought, that conflict remains the South's defining moment, a sociological Super Bowl. Ambivalent about the outcome, we descendents of the losing team will Monday-morning-quarterback it forever.

Admittedly, what I shall say to you next may also sound far-fetched—and you need not take notes, sports fans; this won't be on your exam—nevertheless, a case can be made for a connection between sports and chivalry. In baseball, for example, the pitcher might represent an evil sorcerer who hurls fireballs at a knight standing protectively in front of huddled masses. Sometimes the knight

swats a fireball safely out of sight with the flat side of his sword. Then he gallops around the field of honor, receiving the adulations of the masses.

One such knight dubbed "Sir Babe Ruth" executed his role with extraordinary flair. Legend has it that he sometimes pointed out beforehand the direction in which he would swat the fireball. It is also said that once he did so to fulfill the dying wish of a little boy. That particular fireball can still be seen in the nighttime sky where it appears as a tiny, twinkling star. Go to our University observatory on a visitors night and ask Andy Bell here to point it out to you.

Football players, too, are our latter-day knights. The helmets and padding worn while engaging the enemy is their armor. Depending upon the tides of battle, these knights are constantly standing in defense of their own castle or trying to overrun the enemy's.

So, wouldn't it be appropriate to rename the "Gamecocks," which are really a kind of chicken, as the "Knights?" Think about it—the University of South Carolina Knights! Your preparations for the Clemson-Carolina games could include a display with a bigger-than-life-size pâpier-maché St. George-type knight thrusting his lance into the throat of an evil, fire-breathing tiger-dragon!

Be sure you're staying current with the readings listed on your syllabus. And, if you have some free time, try to see a real baseball game this weekend—I believe that both the University and City of Columbia teams have home games scheduled. Class dismissed.

* * *

Once when I was a little boy, I saw my older cousin Walter in a football game recover a fumble and run it for a decisive touchdown. I also witnessed the reward at game's end for his glorious deed: St. Andrew's prettiest cheerleader bestowed a kiss on his cheek. That chivalrous scene etched itself in my memory. I was proud to be a kinsman of this knight and nurtured fantasies of someday emulating him.

* * *

August of the year I would enter the tenth grade was extremely hot even for Charleston, and very dry. I would always remember the heat and dust of that month because I was trying out for the football team for the first time. I had already procrastinated a year longer than most of my friends. That was because my young and exciting English teacher, Miss Anne Brooks, had recruited me to work on a new literary journal for which she was the faculty advisor. I had doubted I had enough extracurricular time for both athletics and the literary journal, but lovely Miss Brooks could sweet-talk a fellow into almost anything.

I realized if I waited another year, however, I would probably never play organized football. Not wanting to appear unmanly in the eyes of Missy, I felt I had to find time for it. I tried out hoping to be selected for the backfield but was more than satisfied with the second-string lineman position Coach Charlie Conroy gave me.

The competition at St. Andrew's High School was quite keen that year. Accordingly, no new candidate for the team had reason to be too disappointed not to get a "glory" position, a position in which he could personally score points by making touchdowns, kicking fieldgoals, or at least running an occasional game-winning extra point. As it happened, there were a lot of experienced players returning and second-string substitutes saw very little action except during practice scrimmages. Still, all of us were happy to be part of the St. Andrew's

"Rocks" football team. We proudly wore our blue and gold jackets to school every day.

Missy came to all the home games either with her parents or with girlfriends. It was frustrating to end most of the games with my uniform still clean; my spirits would always rise, however, to see Missy at the gate after the games ended cheering the team as it headed for the locker room. She cheered and applauded all of us, but she always had what seemed to be a special smile for me.

In the spring, Missy tried out for the cheerleader squad and, predictably, was successful. She would start in the fall when she entered the ninth grade. She was so vivacious and so full of life, it would have been hard to imagine her not a cheerleader. Here it should be noted that cheerleaders at St. Andrew's High were required to maintain above average grades, as well as to exhibit an engaging personality and the other usual attributes.

Upon entering the eleventh grade, I was almost selected for first string. Coach Conroy came up to me after practice one afternoon and said, "Andy, I kind of think you could handle it. But Tony Edwards outweighs you by twenty pounds and with the schedule we've got this year—well, I need every ounce of meat on that line I can get. But hang in there, son. In this game you never know what's going to happen next. Besides, Edwards is a senior."

As usual, the season opener was with the Summerville Green Wave, our arch-rival and the perennial district champions. Summerville won the toss and elected to receive so that they could start scoring right away. At least, we had the advantage of it being a home game. Over the years the Rocks had won three-fourths of all their home games.

The opening kickoff sent the ball tumbling deep into Green Wave territory where their quarterback scooped it up and was immediately hit so hard by Tony Edwards the ball flew out of his hands and into the end zone. Three Rocks dove to recover the ball, but the Summerville fullback managed to snatch it up on a breathtaking gallop that zigzagged the entire length of the field. True football fans on both sides of the field applauded an

undeniably outstanding carry.

When the commotion subsided the crowd noticed that someone was still on the ground around the Summerville twenty. It was Tony Edwards and he appeared to be writhing in pain. Timeout was called as Coach Conroy and his assistant ran to Tony's side. His leg was twisted at an odd angle and was swelling fast. He was taken from the field on a stretcher.

A referee called for the game to resume. Coach Conroy barked in my direction, "Bell, get your butt in there if you're going to play."

Instantly I jumped up and ran onto the field. Out there I realized my helmet was not on my head and turned to run back to the bench for it. As soon as I turned I saw it coming at me through the air. I caught the helmet and dashed toward our line, reaching my assigned position just as the Summerville team was breaking huddle. The adrenaline was flowing and I was ready to leap at the snap. I felt the football graze the top of my helmet. The deflected ball fell to the outside of the goal post and Summerville was denied their extra point for the first time in three seasons.

That turned out to be the high point of the game for us. Summerville won 20 to 7. Another high point for me, however, came while I was on the bench briefly. The cheerleaders were between routines and Missy ran over to give me a quick hug from behind around my shoulder pads. "Andy, I like football players who can use their heads too. You're a real Rock!" Then she ran back to her group for their next cheer.

Overall, our team played pretty well that night. Afterwards in the locker room Coach Conroy said, "I'm not embarrassed, boys. Summerville is one heck of a team. But, if we can't beat Bishop England next week, I'm going to replace all of you with the junior varsity." Looking at me, he added, "Bell, I'm hoping that extra point block wasn't a fluke. Looks like Edwards is going to be out for a while. Could be out for the rest of the season." And to all of us, he said, "Rest up tomorrow, boys; then on Sunday get your tails to whatever church your family goes to so you can pray we'll beat the britches off those fumbling Catholics next Friday night. And be ready for a hard practice every afternoon from here on out. Or be ready to turn in your uniform. Got it?"

Coach Conroy always led the team in a brief prayer for victory immediately before a game and, if it were close, again at halftime. To me it never seemed appropriate to bother God for something like a football game. Besides, the other team had their own prayers, and you could be certain the Bishop England players would be asking the Blessed Virgin Mary as well as their patron saint to help them win.

Our team had six wins, three losses (Beaufort and, yes, Bishop England were the other two) and a tie (with Walterboro) that season.

* * *

One day the following spring, Missy and I were discussing *Pebbles*, our school literary journal. By that time I was one of the assistant editors and suggested to Missy that she apply to serve on the staff in the fall. Missy then stunned me with the announcement that she was transferring to Ashley Hall, a private school for girls I knew to be expensive and exclusive.

"But why would you want to leave St. Andrew's?" I pleaded. "We have probably the best public school in the state. You won't find more competent or dedicated teachers anywhere. And people say the musical revue Mr. Harper's Drama Club presents every spring is the best thing south of Broadway. Granted, going to school on Rutledge Avenue might have some snob appeal, but is that what you want? You're too—well, the Missy I know is too *natural* to fit in there." If the word "egalitarian" had come to mind at that moment, I would have used it to describe Missy to herself in trying to convince her to remain with me in the public school system.

"Andy," she said, "you know I love St. Andrew's. I'd be happy to stay here forever. But Ashley Hall is where my mother's wanted me to go all along. It's where she went. Dad's always backed me in staying at St. Andrew's, but—but she—we've just learned that my mother has

cancer, Andy, and I want to do this for her."

"Oh, Missy, I'm really sorry. Your mother—your mother is such a lovely lady, and transferring to her alma mater will be a wonderful tribute," I said. Any further effort to persuade Missy not to transfer, I thought, would sound self-serving and would have been inappropriate.

During my senior year I was on the starting lineup, still a bit lighter than Coach Conroy liked his linemen to be, but being a bit faster made up for it. The Rocks had one of their best seasons ever, beginning with a three-field goal 9 to 7 win over Summerville. Week after week we won handily.

The final game of the season turned out to be the most tense. The Blue Devils of North Charleston stayed ahead of us by one touchdown quarter by quarter. Late in the fourth with the score 34 to 28, North Charleston had possession on their forty. The ball was snapped. I rushed through the line at their quarterback but Pete Simpson hit him first and hit him hard enough to pop the ball out of his arm. It was for me a classic case of being in the right place at the right time. The ball fell into my hands as I ran up to the scene of the tackle and I just kept running. The clock ran out as I crossed the goal line, tying the score. My younger neighbor Warren Hancock, a fantastic freshman, was called in to kick the extra point, and we Rocks were district champions.

As the team left the field, Missy was waiting by the gate. She yelled, "Andy!" and ran toward me. Before I could say anything, Missy kissed me squarely on the lips! It was the very first time she had ever done that in public.

Running on toward the locker room, I could hardly wait to shower, get dressed, and see Missy again. She would be waiting for me at the post-game sock hop in the school auditorium. As I stood in the communal shower, which was filled with steam and the noises of victory, I could already see the two of us shagging, then slow dancing cheek to cheek in the dim light. That reminded me I needed to wear a clean jock strap as usual to suppress the inevitable erection. It was the only way I knew to avoid being embarrassed on the dance floor.

After the dance Missy and I would stop by the

Friendly's for thick chocolate milk shakes and hamburgers without onions. Then I would suggest that we drive down to the Battery to watch the submarine races (which, of course, was code for "making out"). This sea wall overlooking Charleston Harbor was our favorite place for parking. At night it was always romantic, and frequent patrol by benevolent police kept it safe. In a perfect world every city, every town, every village would provide for its young lovers a comparable setting for sweet hours of kisses and necking.

A Room of Her Own

On commencement night our school auditorium overflowed with family members and other relatives and friends of the Class of 1957. This was before the era of air conditioning in public schools and the auditorium was stuffy despite all the windows being open. The ceremony had been long but at last was nearing its end. Our white-maned U.S. Congressman, who had become something of a legend in his own lifetime, had reminded us of our debt to state and nation and the need to make patriotic repayment. The salutatorian and valedictorian had made their respective speeches. I, as the class poet laureate, had read an ode I had written in honor of all our teachers over the years. Our beloved principal, Mr. Bernard Harper, had presented our diplomas to us, and all the special awards had been handed out. The time had come for the climactic moment. All the graduates on the stage together with everyone else in the auditorium stood and sang the school alma mater:

Here's to the land that gave us birth,
here's to the flag she flies.
Here's to our sons the best on earth,
here's to her smiling skies.
Here's to our Alma Mater dear,
true as the stars above.
Here's to our faith and honor dear,
here's to the school we love.

St. Andrew's School, St. Andrew's School,
we never shall forget.
The golden haze of student days
is 'round about us yet.

The days of yore will come no more
but through the future years,
the thought of you, so good, so true,
will fill our eyes with tears.
The thought of you, so good, so true,
will fill our eyes with tears.

* * *

Commencement at the end of May marked for many of us on the stage that night the end of twelve years in the public schools of St. Andrew's Parish. My own tenure as a student at each level, elementary, junior high, and high school, had been fulfilling for the most part, providing knowledge and training that would take me as far as my motivation would allow. A St. Andrew's education was a significant intangible asset I would possess always and appreciate more and more as I encountered life's various crises, necessities, and opportunities.

By then Missy's and my relationship was in a holding pattern. We still enjoyed being together, but she seemed to require more distance than a marriage-bound relationship could thrive on. Her transfer to Ashley Hall had introduced her to a lifestyle she was eager to explore. Doors were opening for her. Although Ashley Hall was unable to avail itself of Missy's experience as a cheerleader, her other attributes were quickly recognized. She was elected May Queen. An invitation to the St. Cecilia Ball at last appeared to be in the offing. During a long talk one night she said pointedly, "Andy, before I can think about settling down with *any* man, I have to know who *I* am."

To have labelled her a social climber, however, would not have been altogether accurate. Mainly, Missy was curious, as all of us are—or should be.

That my love for Missy was more than imagination, there could be no doubt; that I wanted someday to be married to her, I was certain. Furthermore, I was mature enough to realize I could only lose her by not letting her loose. Metaphorically speaking, perhaps, like Virginia Woolf, she had reached the stage in her life of needing a

room of her own. I decided to join the army and wait for her at what I hoped would be a fruitful distance.

By then Mrs. Brinson's cancer was in remission. On the day I was inducted and left for Fort Gordon, Georgia, to begin basic training, Mr. and Mrs. Brinson and Missy were in Virginia for Bubba's graduation from the Episcopal School for Boys. That morning at the Greyhound Bus Station on Society Street, my parents saw me off with hugs and fond farewells which did little to take my mind off Missy.

* * *

Later I was reassigned to Germany, flying into Frankfurt on February 14. The preceding week had been sufficiently hectic to provide an excuse for not having mailed a Valentine's Day card to Missy, but the oversight still troubled me. Besides that gnawing concern, I had never seen so much snow before. The sight of it chilled my Southern psyche.

In Frankfurt I was given a train ticket to Augsburg and orders to report to 11th Airborne Division headquarters there. On the train a pretty fraulein with long red hair, who spoke English very well and with an engaging accent, and who must have thought I looked painfully lonely, initiated a conversation. We talked for hours. I regretted having to say "*Auf Wiedersehen*" when the train arrived in Augsburg. She reminded me so much of Missy, it hurt. The next morning found me among about twenty replacements in the back of an army truck (the kind the troops called a "deuce and a half") headed down the *Autobahn* toward my regiment in Munich.

* * *

Although I missed her, Missy's letters came regularly during most of my first year in Germany and brought with them a sense of closeness, an assurance that our young love would survive and somehow be strengthened by our separation. By the time Munich's Oktoberfest was held, Missy was in her senior year at Ashley Hall; and, although she was having casual dates with pimply boys whom I knew were no threat to our relationship, she opened every letter with the reassuring words "I'm available." This was a whimsical reference to a popular song of the same title we listened to while cuddling most of the final week I had at home before leaving for Germany.

After I had been there eight or nine months, I began to sense subtle changes in the tone of Missy's letters. When I asked her about this, she assured me it was just a matter of being distracted with the academic requirements of a senior year in a demanding school. The real reason for Missy's distraction was revealed in her next letter:

> Dear Andy,
>
> I'm no longer available. Something has happened I cannot explain because when it began it was supposed to be strictly platonic. There were sweet thoughts of you every day and every night. But one morning I woke up and realized I was in love with someone else. We would like to be married soon but I'm sure my parents will insist on my finishing college first. (I've definitely decided to enroll at Sweetbriar and major in biology. I'll need that to get into medical school.) Besides, my fiancé has two more years at The Citadel, then his ROTC commitment unless he can get a deferment to work on his M.B.A. It's likely to be a long engagement.
>
> Please forgive me for letting this happen. And please know that I would never have planned it. You are and will always be a special person to me. (Which is why I often reread a poem in the Sara Teasdale collection you gave me one Christmas—I'll enclose a copy so you'll know what I mean.) I fervently hope our friendship will continue as long as we live.

I'm sure that when the time is right, you will meet the right person for you. She'll be a very lucky girl!

We heard from Bubba last night. He's still doing very well at Sewanee and is active in Canterbury Club. I'm betting he'll announce in one of his letters soon that he wants to go to seminary after leaving Sewanee. Can you imagine that—my brother, Bubba Brinson, a priest? Well, I guess the two of you keep in touch (and I hope you always will) and so this probably isn't news to you.

Stay wonderful.

Affections,
Missy

The Coin

Into my heart's treasury
I slipped a coin
That time cannot take
Nor a thief purloin—
Oh, better than the minting
Of a gold-crowned king
Is the safe-kept memory
Of a lovely thing.

Sara Teasdale

P.S.: Andy, each of our times together was a *lovely thing.*

M.

Wedding

My undergraduate marriage to Lake was brief. Our sophomoric union lasted eleven weeks, which was less than a season, less than the length of an ordinary college semester. It had been more like an interlude of the imagination than real life, an adolescent soap opera of romance and rejection, fiery infatuation and familial interference. If I had had my wits about me, rather than writing the several cathartic poems few people will ever read, I would have scripted the experience for afternoon television. And had my artistic integrity been challenged later for having produced such pulp, I could have simply and sincerely justified it as juvenilia.

The truth is, on one level, Lake and I were like two curious children who live next door to each other in an idyllic neighborhood and who in a precocious moment decide to play house. In their innocent play these children interact quite happily. Their paradise ends only when the parent of one of them summarily calls her child in from play, afraid, perhaps, that the game is about to go too far, that, instead of just making mud pies, the children are about to bite into the apple pie of forbidden knowledge.

It is also true, however, that on the level of reality our connubial union went quite beyond all parameters of play. It had been consummated, formalized, and, in some sense, reconsummated on the day of our elopement. Furthermore, over the course of the following eleven weeks, the consummation had been confirmed repeatedly. This was reality, a reality which could become as sticky as the semen carrying the sperm that overcame considerable odds to swell her belly. Unequivocally, ours qualified as a legally recognized relationship. As such it could only be officially ended on a specific date by the legal dissolution represented by a "d" word, a word more profane in its sound than a whole mouthful of "damns," a word denoting an end often more devastating than death to those against whom it is initiated: *divorce.*

* * *

Because of my divorce, when Missy and I began making plans for our wedding, it was necessary for me to petition the bishop of our diocese for permission to be married in the Church. After filing such a petition there follows an obligatory meeting with one's bishop to discuss the matter. The addressee of my petition, of course, was Missy's great-uncle, the Rt. Rev. Matthew Middleton Jackson, then in his fifteenth year as Bishop of the Diocese of South Carolina. Shortly before the appointed time for our meeting, I left my office in the ivy-covered Department of English building at the College of Charleston, where I taught freshman composition and creative writing, and walked the several blocks up Coming Street to the Cathedral of St. Luke and St. Paul.

Bishop Jackson's headquarters were in the close beside the cathedral. He was happy for Missy and me and greeted me warmly. As we sat in his study, he looked at me over the top of his reading glasses and said with mock incredulousness, "Now, young man, what's this you ask? You want to marry my niece, my precious, paragon-of-purity niece? Aren't you an 'Andy-come-lately' to the Church? And is there any truth to the rumor that you write x-rated poems?"

"The answer to your first question, at least your first nonrhetorical question, depends on which church you mean, Your Grace," I replied, enjoying the repartee anyone favored by Bishop Jackson could have with him. "As the record will show, I was baptized at First Baptist Church when I was eight years old. I was a member there and later at Ashley River Baptist for the next eight years. But, as you yourself have acknowledged, Bishop,

'Baptists make the best Episcopalians.'"

As soon as I cited that frequently repeated expression, an adage so cherished by certain converted Episcopalians like myself, I recognized the possible pun on the word "make." I hoped the good bishop had not.

I continued, "As for being a poet, I confess that the rumor has some substance. But, in defense, I must assert that none of my poems are pornographic and only a few may be slightly more sensual than the Song of Solomon. More relevantly, Bishop, the editor of our diocesan newsletter has found several sufficiently innocuous to publish. I trust you read *Jubilate Deo* regularly and saw them there."

"Andy, at the risk of swelling your head, I'll admit not only to having read and enjoyed them, but also to having used one, 'Lenten Meditation,' to open my Ash Wednesday sermon this year:

> *Wednesday of the smudge, and I*
> *with forehead more unblemished*
> *than soul make the supreme*
> *sacrifice of giving up nothing:*

My memory's failing, son—how does the rest of it go?"

I finished my poem for him:

> *To roam for forty days,*
> *carrying no cross*
> *to cover my nakedness*
> *and foregoing this sacred*
> *serendipity of spring;*
> *to walk in the wilderness*
> *of total self-indulgence—*
> *understood only by God.*

"That's a powerful poem, Andy, poignant and challenging. Wish I'd written it."

"Thank you very much, Bishop. Anyhow, your niece seduced me into Anglicanism when we both were still in high school. And it's quite likely we would've been

married in the Church years ago had Missy not been mesmerized by the first Citadel cadet uniform to walk by her after I joined the army and was assigned to Germany."

The bishop sighed and replied, "Yes, that was an unfortunate turn of events, wasn't it? There you were off doing your part to help keep the world safe for democracy, and Missy keeping questionable company with a draft-dodging cadet!"

We discussed various subjects for an hour to allow the bishop an opportunity, I suppose, to assess the state of my spiritual life as well as my mental and emotional stability. Then he said, "Well, son, I guess I'll have to grant your petition. Missy is a strong-willed young woman, and I wouldn't want to have to face her if I couldn't approve it. In any event, I do think her decisions are right more often than they're wrong, and the decision to marry you is a case in point. In all seriousness, I think you both have made felicitous decisions."

"Then we have your blessing, Bishop?"

"Without qualification. I'll have Lisa, my secretary, prepare the proper letter to make it official. When does Missy—I should say, when do *y'all* want the ceremony?"

Beaming, I answered, "Missy thinks a sunny Saturday in October would be ideal. Naturally, we want to be married at Old St. Andrew's Church, and we're hoping that you will participate along with Father Collins, our new rector out there, and, of course, Bubba."

"Tell Missy that the weather is controlled at a higher level in the hierarchy than mine; however, I would be delighted to take part in the nuptials and will be praying for sunny skies. By the way, have you discussed this with Kevin Collins yet?"

"Well, Sir, we thought talking with him before talking with you may've been a bit too presumptuous. But, hoping for the best with regard to my petition, Missy and I did presume to make an appointment to meet with Kevin next week."

* * *

I have never enjoyed any ceremony, party, or other

festivity as much as Missy's and my wedding. It was held at four o'clock in the afternoon on an Indian summer Saturday at the end of October, a perfect day for a new beginning.

After the rehearsal dinner at the Lodge Alley Inn the night before, I did not see Missy again until shortly before the ceremony was to begin. I was waiting for her under an ancient oak in the churchyard when she emerged from the parish hall. In that extraordinary moment, the effect of seeing her was electric; it was like being smitten for the first time: She appeared as beatific as she was beautiful. It was one of those particularly memorable moments which are the raw material of poetry.

Of course, I had not previously seen Missy in her wedding dress, so the effect was all the more stunning. It was off-white, classically simple, and set off dramatically by the bold tartan sash worn over her shoulder. Pinned to the sash over her heart was the traditional *luckenbooth* I had given her to mark our engagement. The bouquet she carried in one hand was a cluster of colors complementing the tartan: a blend of burgundy, several shades of green, and bright yellow. A matching garland crowned her with grace.

Specifically, Missy wore an *Ancient MacMillan* tartan inasmuch as the Bells are a sept of Clan MacMillan in the Highlands of Scotland. Wearing the tartan symbolized a pledge of her allegiance to my clan. It was a commitment of fidelity which could not be articulated better than by Ruth's prototypical pledge to Naomi, a promise preserved for posterity in the Old Testament book, as beautiful as it is brief, that bears her name.

I stood speechless under the tree as Missy, maintaining eye contact each step of the way, walked toward me. Then, still looking into my eyes, she took my hand tenderly in hers and softly, sweetly, convincingly paraphrased Ruth's immortal words: "Andy, entreat me not to leave thee, or to turn away from following after thee; for where thou goest, I will go; and where thou lodgest, I will lodge: thy clan shall be my clan, and thy God, my God."

Mr. Brinson paid further deference to my family's

Scottish heritage by arranging for Charleston's most reknown bagpiper to play at the wedding. When it was time for the ceremony to begin, Captain Alexander McIntosh piped Missy and me from under the oak and across the churchyard, fading out as she and I entered the church. At the instant of our entry, the organ accompanied by trumpet and tympany began the procession, for which we had chosen the "Hornpipe" movement from Handel's *Water Music.*

Our order of service followed closely the one in the Episcopal Book of Common Prayer with only minor variations that were important to us. An exhortation was followed by the betrothal, which in turn was followed by a poem, "The Bed," from the works of George Garrett. This aptly titled poem was beautifully read by our dear friend Eliza Summers, an accomplished poet herself.

Then there was the Epistle (I Corinthians 13:1-13) and the song "Panis Angelicus" sung by a member of the church choir. Everyone then stood for the Holy Gospel (John 15:9-12), read by David Rosenthall, who happened to be a Messianic Jew and Eliza's fiancé. David ended his reading with the coda-like phrase, "The Gospel of the Lord."

Antiphonally, the people said, "Praise to you, Lord Christ," and sat down.

When everyone was settled, Bubba stepped up into the quaint, colonial pulpit to deliver his homily. He began by reading another passage from John, that first part of the second chapter which refers to the wedding feast at Cana of Galilee, the occasion of Jesus' first miracle when He changed water into wine. Bubba asserted that Jesus' presence and actions at Cana constituted a significant endorsement of the institution of marriage.

He was in character when he concluded his homily by saying this: "And like that divine wine, a good marriage should be slightly intoxicating, a foretaste of heaven. Analogous to the traditional 'happy hour' so many of us whiskey 'palians look forward to for refreshment at the end of a difficult day, your union is meant to help you get through life, a journey which is much more difficult when taken alone than with a compatible companion.

"Andrew, Mary-Martha, this is your Cana. We have invoked the presence of the spirit of the Master Winemaker, and in this joyful hour we humbly beseech of Him this blessing: May you never be satiated with the miracle that is your marriage, as long as you both shall live."

The marriage itself was then performed by Father Collins with more prayers and blessings. Bishop Jackson was chief celebrant for Holy Communion, with all baptized believers present invited to partake, following the bride and groom.

The stirring recessional was "The Rejoicing" from Handel's *Royal Fireworks Music*. Missy and I would be fans of Handel for the rest of our lives. Together or apart we would listen to the *Water Music*, the *Fireworks Music*, *Messiah*, and other compositions of his repeatedly.

As we exited the church Captain McIntosh was waiting to pipe us across the parking lot to a car covered with the traditional graffiti and decorations. Missy and I snuggled on the back seat while David and Eliza chauffeured us into the city for the reception. As the procession drove along Ashley River Road and under its state-protected canopy of oaks, Captain McIntosh rode right behind us in the back of Bubba's convertible. Its top was down and he played sprightly all the way. He also played at the reception, which was held at Hibernian Hall in deference to the Brinsons' Irish origins.

The reception was memorable: it was a festive blend of lavish feast, including a variety of such exotic treats as haggis and she-crab soup, a party with music for dancing, two family reunions, and more. When guests began getting ready to leave, Missy and I went through the traditional tossing of her bouquet and garter belt. Eliza caught the bouquet. Bubba "sort of" caught the garter belt after some other eligible bachelors around him batted it in his direction. But playfully he insisted his catch was invalid and that it was unsecmly for him even to hold an item which had been worn so intimately, even so briefly, by his own sister. He then made me toss the lacy elastic talisman again so that David Rosenthall could catch it. David and Eliza beamed as they gave each other a quick hug and received a round of congratulatory

applause.

Missy and I enjoyed the reception at least as much as any of the guests and probably stayed later than is customary for a new bride and groom. Finally, however, after my father reminded me of our schedule, she and I tore ourselves away from the fun and let my parents drive us to the airport for a purposely mysterious honeymoon flight to wherever it was we were going. Actually, we were headed for St. Thomas in the Virgin Islands, but shared this secret only with our parents, fearing that the very name of our destination would have occasioned a lot of ribbing from our friends. We arrived at the airport just in time to check our baggage and run through the gate.

Minutes later the plane rolled down the runway and lifted smoothly into the starry sky. Almost instantly we were far above even the city's highest steeples and after another moment the marshes and the woods that had made childhood in Charleston so special. We held hands. We were pleased to have our beautiful wedding behind us and the rest of our lives before us.

At last I felt sufficiently confident of our relationship to lay to rest an old restraint. For the first time I asked her, "Missy, do you remember that day in Bubba's bedroom—it was a hot summer day, you were about eleven. There was a rotating red light and some jazz and you treated me to my very first striptease?"

Her answer was an unconstrained laugh loud enough to attract the attention of all the other passengers around us. When she had regained most of her composure, through the continuing girlish giggles she said, "What a wicked memory you have, Andrew Bell! It was unfair of you not to disclose it before we took final vows."

"Do you mean my 'wicked memory' or your wicked striptease?"

"You *know* what I mean," she said with another giggle, cuffing my shoulder.

"By the way, I liked the sound of your real name when Bubba used it in his homily. I think I'm going to call you 'Mary-Martha' from now on."

"You do and you'll have seen your last striptease."

"In which case we could call you 'Mary Magdalene' to

signify your reformation," I kidded. "You could even emulate your new namesake by washing my feet and drying them with your long red hair."

"Andy, I'm *warning* you—you're bordering on sacrilege and I'll have to report you to Uncle Middleton."

"Then let it remain 'Missy,' Missy."

To use the idiom of fairy tales, we were ready to live happily forever after.

* * *

I planned to surprise Missy on the trip with the exciting news of a job offer with the U.S. Commission on Civil Rights in Washington, D.C. Actually, I had already accepted the offer, and I should have known Missy well enough to realize that making such a decision unilaterally was a mistake. Except for a honeymoon, vacation, or other absence of finite duration, leaving Charleston was one of the last things she would ever want to do. Notwithstanding the fact that she had had many Ashley Hall friends at Sweet Briar College, Missy was often homesick during her four years there—although I happen to believe it was as much for the cadet as it was for the city—and said she never again wanted to be away from Charleston for that long. Among other things, leaving Charleston now would complicate and could delay her plans to begin medical school.

I waited until the morning after our arrival in St. Thomas to broach this sensitive subject. We argued. We made passionate love again. She acquiesced.

Separation

Missy and I separated on a Sunday in September. I remember that day well. For a long time I remembered it too well, perhaps, for my own well-being. It was only the eve of autumn and already the leaves were turning. After a cooler-than-usual summer, the air was heavy with hints of an early winter. Soon, the deciduous trees of Northern Virginia would be ablaze and, too soon—always too soon—after that, they would be bare.

As had become our custom by the second year we were back in Reston, the family slept late and skipped church. We were nominal members of St. Catherine's Episcopal Church in Arlington. St. Catherine's congregation was warm and caring; its handsome rector seemed to be a very compassionate man. Nevertheless, Missy and I soon lost much of our enthusiasm for the church after detecting subtle signs that this priest harbored more than a pastoral interest in her, an unwelcome interest which we did not know how to discourage without risking a conceivably undeserved offense to him and mortifying embarrassment to us. Accordingly, we simply chose the course of least resistance; besides, the distance from Reston provided a ready, rational excuse to become lax in our attendance. Incidentally, I would learn later that the rector of St. Catherine's eventually found someone in his flock to replace his faithful and attractive but too intense wife—her slender, easygoing best friend, whom he married and now lived with in the diocese of one of the Church's most controversial bishops. Naturally, hearing that triggered a memory of Bubba's earlier confession to me of his own involvement with Priscilla. I began to wonder if this phenomenon were becoming endemic in their profession

or in our denomination.

Separation Sunday breakfast for Missy and me was coffee and doughnuts; Robin and Paul had orange juice and sugar-coated cereal as well as doughnuts, of course. Those powdered doughnuts were Paul's favorite food and, given the inherent selfishness of their parents' plans for the day, the innocent children of this about-to-be halved household deserved to be indulged. Nevertheless, Missy and I were remiss and would regret not preparing a more nourishing meal on this occasion. By late afternoon all four of us would be needing the psychic strength our bodies could have been assimilating from hot grits or oatmeal, fresh eggs, sausage, bacon, or ham, and buttered whole wheat toast. Predictably, neither Missy nor I found much strength or satisfaction in this sorry repast of expediency.

After eating, I read the *Washington Post* while Missy washed a couple of loads of laundry. She was devoting what was left of the morning to packing her and the kids' clothes. Robin and Paul were playing outside by themselves. Jessica and Ray, respectively their best friends and closest playmates, probably were where Robin and Paul should have been at that hour, in Sunday School.

"Missy, as I said, I'd be happy to help you do anything you can use help with—not happy, really, but certainly willing."

"I know, sweetheart, but most of what we're taking today is already packed and this won't take long. I assume you'll help me load it all in the wagon after we get back from the park."

"Sure, hon," I said, resuming my reading of the op-ed page and musing on the irony of our still using pet terms of endearment in the final hours of cohabitation.

Our last lunch together was literally a picnic; figuratively, it was a deathwatch, if not a wake, for our marriage. We picked up some Pappy's Fried Chicken and carried it to a Fairfax County park nearby. After eating, but reluctant to leave, we lingered at the table, sipping lemonade and watching Robin and Paul romp with a neighbor's kids on the gentle, grassy slopes. And we rehashed once more the dialog that had become a litany. With minor variations, it is one chanted by men and women in every city and community in America.

"Missy, you *know* you don't have to leave. Why don't you change your mind? It's still not too late."

"What about you, Andy, won't you change yours? I *want* to stay. Make it possible for me. All you have to do is just give me a promise that we'll get out of this overpopulated, overpolluted, crime-ridden, capital of everything that's wrong with America—that we'll get out, all four of us together, by some reasonable deadline. Just give me a firm date that would allow me to start med school by next fall. It really seems so simple to me, Andy." And with a touch of levity to lighten the mood, she added, "Sweetheart, I may be too old already to specialize in pediatrics; soon I'll be too old even for geriatrics!"

"Well, hon, this sounds a lot like a conversation we've had a few times before, doesn't it? You know I want you to stay, very much. And you know you'd have my full support, my loving encouragement, all that, if you went to school here. But, most of all, I want you to stay because it's the right thing to do and to stay without any unreasonable conditions. I can't say that on 'x' date I'll cease to be concerned about the poor, the oppressed, the homeless, the—"

"What's unreasonable about asking for a *normal* family life for ourselves? God knows, I'm proud of what you've done for the poor and oppressed here, but it's time to go home, Andy! It's time to get back to Charleston! Washington isn't our home. And Reston—Reston is just a very expensive camp for transients. Charleston has homelessness and poverty, too. You could stay busy there with useful projects the rest of our lives. And the part-time position my father's friend offered in the Office of Human Affairs would be perfect: It would let you continue to work with groups you want to help as well as allow you ample time for your poetry, your essays—you claim you never have enough time for your writing."

"Missy, it's not the same. My work here helps people all over the country."

"Are you so irreplaceable—or is the importance of

your position just essential to your ego?"

"That's not fair, Missy, and you know it."

"You're right, it's not fair. I'm sorry I said it. It's just that at this point I'm too frustrated to be fair. I'm hurting inside, Andy."

I waited for a moment, then said in a softer voice, "I can't beg you to stay, but please know I want you to."

This tableau produced a strong sense of *déjà vu.* The reason, I suppose, was a recollection of our relationship in high school, the memory of how it felt to have to let her loose to preclude losing her altogether . . . .

"You know how to reach me if you change your mind. Or if you just want to call sometime to say you still love us," Missy said, her voice beginning to break as four children, temporarily bored with romping and ready for more chocolate chip cookies, ran up to the table.

When we returned to what within hours would no longer be *our* home, I helped Missy finish packing and loading her almost new Volvo station wagon, a cranberry-colored extravagance given a few months earlier to curry her favor. Soon it was full with her share of the pewter plates, salad bowls, blankets, and the children—both of them, which was all of them: we had resolved not to compound our failure to survive as a couple; we were determined not to separate Robin and Paul from each other. (And we had simply told them they all were going for an extended visit with their grandparents in Charleston—too long for their daddy to be away from his job.) As for splitting fond, mutually-held memories, we knew of no way to divide without destroying these, which was unthinkable, and agreed to permanent copossession.

With the September sun glinting the red hair she had again let grow long to please me, Missy and I stood beside her wagon and kissed. Unhurried, it was a long, tender, bittersweet kiss. Still in each other's embrace, Missy said, "I can't believe that in a few minutes we won't be living together anymore."

Squeezing, then slowly letting go of her, I promised, "I'll be calling."

Missy opened the door and sat in the wagon. For a long moment she just sat and stared through the windshield as if she didn't know what to do next. From the back seat with a slobbery kiss, there was a plaintive farewell from my fairhaired son: "I wish you were coming with us." Paul, with all the wisdom of his three years, had voiced the simplest and, no doubt, best solution to an endemic adult dilemma.

Robin, four years older than Paul and perceiving, I shall always believe, the significance of their trip, sat in heartbreaking silence, pretending to be engrossed in the book she held with slightly trembling hands. It was the kind of silence no caring parent wishes for a seven-year-old daughter. It was a silence which encompassed many feelings, not the least of which was a sadness to be leaving her school, Lake Anne Elementary, her friends and friendly teachers, just two weeks into the second grade, a sadness she bravely and magnanimously kept to herself, sensing her mother and father were already heavily weighted with the guilt of their intransigence.

The mere mention of Lake Anne Elementary never fails to remind me of the touching note Robin's teacher sent home with her on her last day there. It simply said she would be missed and conveyed the hope she would be happy in her new school. Between those sincere lines, moreover, I read an equally sincere sympathy for our family—no doubt one of the many in Reston and all over America whom teachers saw following tragically similar scripts. I still have and shall always treasure that note, as well as a haloed image of the teacher who wrote it. I have never met her—I could never summon the courage to face her . . . .

Missy finally turned the ignition key. A cassette had been left in the tape player and "The Rejoicing" from Handel's *Royal Fireworks Music* erupted from the speakers. This piece, of course, had been used as the recessional at our wedding, and the irony was poignant. Missy quickly pushed the eject button. She glanced up at me and began backing the wagon into a turn. Then she moved it forward slowly through the parking lot, stopping before making a left turn onto Moorings Drive, where

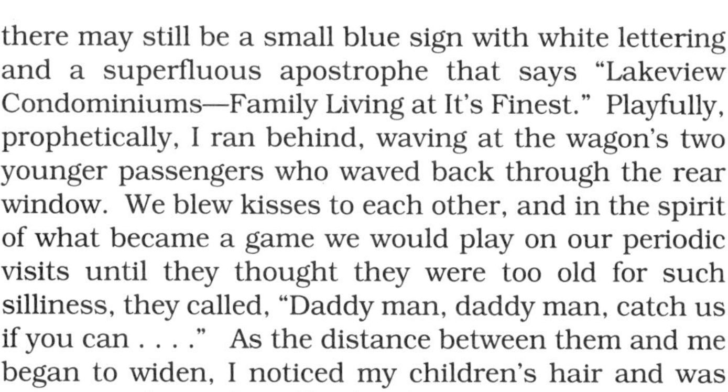

there may still be a small blue sign with white lettering and a superfluous apostrophe that says "Lakeview Condominiums—Family Living at It's Finest." Playfully, prophetically, I ran behind, waving at the wagon's two younger passengers who waved back through the rear window. We blew kisses to each other, and in the spirit of what became a game we would play on our periodic visits until they thought they were too old for such silliness, they called, "Daddy man, daddy man, catch us if you can . . . ." As the distance between them and me began to widen, I noticed my children's hair and was momentarily comforted by the observation that they were at least as blond as I.

It was only a short drive to the highway. The widening distance quickly became a gulf, then they were gone. The single word on an orange sign in front of the Gulf Service Station on the corner mocked me. I must have stood mesmerized in the middle of the road for several minutes before another car approached and startled me with a toot from its horn. I turned and walked away as if I were leaving a battlefield in defeat. Egotistically speaking, it was the end of an era.

(What I have just tried to describe in prose is something I have never been able to say in a poem—the intensity of poetry makes the very process too painful. Nevertheless, a dear friend and fellow poet with whom I shared my grief was able to say what I could not in "The Grieving":

It was stupid of him
to let it happen.
If he could have known,
had even a notion of it,
he would not have agreed
for her to leave,
would not have helped her
load the wagon.
He might have lain down
in front of the tires,
cut open his hands
and feet,

slit his chest,
perhaps showed her his heart,
dropped to his knees
and begged her
to stay.

And she would have then.

He might have said,
wait until winter passes
when the beds are not as lonely.
He might have said,
look
these are the plants we
bought in our first year.
He might have said,
tell me what part of you is restless
and I will sing to it.

And she would have stayed.

Yes, if only I had sung to that part of her which was "restless," Missy might have stayed.)

In my mind, I saw Missy and the children in the cranberry-colored Volvo turning right on Virginia Route 7 and taking it to Tyson's Corner. Robin would no longer be pretending to read; rather, she would be gazing out the window at nothing, or curled into a corner of the back seat hoping to fall asleep, later to wake and be relieved to know the trip was just a bad dream. Paul, no less sensitive, but much more pragmatic, would be making the most of the trip. He liked cars and trucks of all kinds and would be excited by all those he saw.

Off to the left and quite visible from the highway would be a mammoth shopping center with a large Bloomingdale's in front. This store had become Missy's favorite place to shop for the stylish clothes in which she always looked so good, so sweet, and, when she taught, so professional. Her mood would be too heavy, however, for her to take note of what they were passing, and it would not occur to her that at that very moment she was

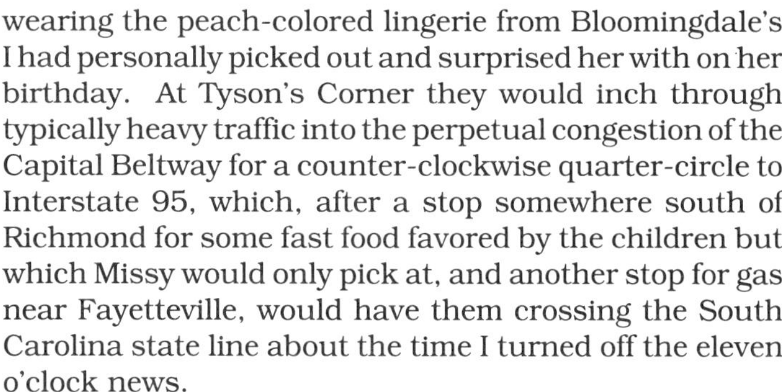

wearing the peach-colored lingerie from Bloomingdale's I had personally picked out and surprised her with on her birthday. At Tyson's Corner they would inch through typically heavy traffic into the perpetual congestion of the Capital Beltway for a counter-clockwise quarter-circle to Interstate 95, which, after a stop somewhere south of Richmond for some fast food favored by the children but which Missy would only pick at, and another stop for gas near Fayetteville, would have them crossing the South Carolina state line about the time I turned off the eleven o'clock news.

Returning to the condo, I found it visibly as it had been a half-hour earlier; but there was a profound, almost palpable difference in its aura. Curiously, it was still incongruously fully furnished. Missy had made arrangements to stay with her parents—who were willing to offer their hospitality, but not their blessing, to a cherished, however headstrong daughter leaving a beloved son-in-law—for an extended period. Also, and very generously, she did not want to leave me to live like a suburban hermit.

I stood at the foot of my children's bunk bed and picked up the stuffed panda Paul had told me he was leaving to keep me company until they returned. I noticed that Robin had drawn for me a picture of horses with colored chalk on her blackboard, and had inscribed it "To Daddy, Loving you wherever I will be. Robin." Then, like a wave of nausea or vertigo, I felt myself falling into a vast chasm of unconnectedness, a discontinuity of physical, mental, and emotional functioning. And this was only the beginning, the first hour. In the months to come, months which would bring to Virginia the harshest winter in its history, nuances of any kind of warmth would be rare. Thousands of water pipes would burst. Scores of shops and schools would close. Many motor vehicles would be inoperable for weeks; my own car could not be cranked for days on end. My spirit would freeze. In due course I would get to know very well the absolute emptiness analogous to absolute zero—neither possesses any energy whatsoever—the emptiness that lies on the other side of loneliness, far beyond the reach of all light

and human laughter, embracing her as I would an illicit lover with whom there could be no future.

Santa Fe

One effect of the separation I should have foreseen but failed to was the deterioration of my hitherto highly-praised performance for the Civil Rights Commission. I had assumed I would be able to continue to lose myself in my job, to continue to wallow in the role of workaholic, to continue to immerse myself so completely in professional duties and responsibilities as to be immune to every form of psychic pain. Such an assumption seemed reasonable in view of my position on the cutting edge of certain significant developments in the civil rights arena. As it happened, during the period leading into the separation, I was engrossed in authoring for the Commission a position paper on the issue of civil rights for the homeless, which my director termed "unprecedented" and "critically important." (As an independent agency of the Executive Branch, we could only state our "position"; we lacked legal authority to set official government policy.) At least for the length of my typically long work day, I tried to convince myself, I could sublimate the emotional turmoil. I had not wanted to tell my colleagues or my department director, Jerry Stender, about the separation; nevertheless, it was naive of me to think my feelings about Missy's and my parting of ways could be hidden behind the facade of a business-as-usual demeanor. Within a couple of weeks Jerry as well as other close colleagues and associates had perceived that I was profoundly distracted.

"Hey, Andy," he said as he came into my office one Monday morning carrying two cups of coffee, one of which he set in front of me before sitting and continuing to speak, "it's Jerry, your boss. Remember me? Where the heck are you? I recognize your pin-striped and

corduroy suits walking into the office in the mornings. Right now I see your L.L. Bean shirt and, looks like, Episcopal Church-crest tie under a face that looks like yours on the other side of your desk. But your mind's been somewhere else lately, hasn't it? Rest assured, I have no complaints about your work—at least nothing major. Those few changes I had to make in your draft last week were just to tone it down a bit to keep the White House happy—certainly nothing to worry about. If I had to do your performance evaluation today rather than month after next, I wouldn't think twice about giving you the same 'outstanding' I've been pleased to give—that is, you yourself have earned for the past two years. But that could change, Andy, and, for the time being, more as a fellow human being than as your supervisor, I'll just ask if there's anything going on you care to talk about with me. If there's not, I'll just say, 'Keep up the good work,' and leave you to it."

Jerry was a very nice guy, a straightforward, unpretentious native of an unpretentious state, West Virginia. Notwithstanding occasional fits of frustration no one in the Federal work force is totally immune to, he was congenial and about as close a friend as one's supervisor could be in Federal Civil Service. He was also an elder in his Presbyterian church in Chevy Chase, Maryland, as well as a scoutmaster for his son's Boy Scout troop. I knew he merited my confidence.

"Well, Jerry," I said, "since you've asked, I'll unload it on you." I paused, took a deep breath, then said, "The proverbial bottom has dropped out from beneath me: Missy's gone, the children too. She left two Sunday's ago. It was sort of by mutual consent, I guess, but afterwards, almost immediately, I realized it was a terrible mistake." And I proceeded to share with him my sad story. "She never thought we'd be away from Charleston this long. And, initially, I may have unintentionally misled her. To tell you the truth, Jerry, I didn't expect to be working here this long either. While I anticipated the work would be worthwhile and fulfilling for some finite period, I really didn't expect to find something I could be happy doing for the rest of my work life. If you have any suggestions, my

heart is humble and my ears are open." Finished with what I had to say, I felt drained and took another deep breath while Jerry made an empathic grimace.

My director was a natural counselor. He had listened carefully, now he spoke compassionately: "Andy, I hear you saying your life's been turned upside down and you're hurting. It also sounds like your hindsight may be telling you that you could've prevented Missy's departure. Naturally, that adds guilt to your grief, doesn't it? Andy, most men have experienced something similar at some point in their lives to what you're going through, and we can have real empathy with each other. In the final analysis, however, each of us has to do his own suffering. This is so true it has become a cliche: Every man has his own cross to bear; sooner or later, everybody goes to a Golgotha."

With a wan smile I said, "Gee, Jerry, that sounds tainted with Presbyterian predestination, but I certainly don't doubt the validity of it."

"Good, Andy, because you would do so at your own peril. Listen, since you invite specific suggestions, I'll just say I think you should consider taking advantage of the agency's 'troubled employee' program. The liaison person for the agency is the EEO officer, Margaret Lee. Maggie is a good soul and has a reputation for being helpful. If you ask her, I'm sure she can put you in touch with some kind of counselor who should be able to help you sort things out.

"The counselors who participate in the program, I am led to understand, are under contract with the government. So it doesn't cost the employee an arm and a leg to get some help—I understand the going rate now for a fifty-minute hour with a psychiatrist in Washington is comparable to a whole day's pay for a GS-13! Can you believe that? I think that's just obscene. Our country's health care system—and I mean mental care as well as physical—is way out of kilter. Anyhow, why don't you just talk with Maggie and check out her program."

"I'll think it over, Jerry. And, by the way, I couldn't agree more with your assessment that our health care system is 'out of kilter.' One chapter in this paper I'm

writing on the homeless addresses the deplorable state of health care delivery to them as well as to other disadvantaged groups. But the system's becoming so very inadequate that there's a silver lining: I'll be bold enough to predict that within a few years there will be a genuinely national debate on this issue, that congressional and, perhaps, even presidential elections will be determined by it, and eventually the country will see the light and adopt a system very much like Canada's."

"You're dreaming, Andy, but it's a beautiful dream—that's one of the things I like about you. Too often, the longer most of us are in this business, the less we dream. Well, I've got a meeting with Commissioner Fielding in a few minutes. You know where my office is and you have my home phone number. Don't hesitate to let me know if there's anything I can do—and just between you and me, I've been through this too. Hang in there," he encouraged, extending his hand for mine and giving it a firm, friendly shake.

"Thanks, Jerry," I said gratefully, "for bringing both the coffee and the solace."

He was walking out of my office when an impulse stopped him. He turned and said, "Nancy's making crab cakes for dinner tonight. I know she'd be happy for you to join us. Interested?"

"I'd be a fool to turn down Nancy's famous Maryland crab cakes," I answered. "I'll be there, so please tell your lovely wife I haven't eaten in two weeks."

I went to see the EEO officer the same day. In general terms and as briefly as possible, I outlined my situation. I heard myself use words and phrases like "domestic crisis," "distracted," "depressed," "insomnia," "reports overdue," and "upcoming annual performance evaluation."

Ms. Lee, like Jerry, exuded empathy. She, too, listened carefully, then she explained how the "troubled employee" program worked. It would not cost me very much out of pocket, for example, and, if necessary, I could be authorized administrative leave to go to counseling sessions. The program sounded too good to be true. I asked her to enroll me.

When I left Ms. Lee's office a little later, I had an appointment she had arranged for me at the District of Columbia Counseling Center the following afternoon. The way the program worked, any one of the counselors on duty and available at that time could be assigned my case.

The next day I took a taxi to the counseling center. The address was in a transitional neighborhood near the Hilton Hotel where President Ronald Reagan would later be shot (and then rushed to the same place several blocks up Pennsylvania Avenue from the White House, George Washington University Hospital, where my daughter Robin was born and at whose medical school I had hoped in vain her mother would enroll). The building itself was run-down. I began to have second thoughts. Inside, I waited for an uninterested, gum-chewing receptionist to complete what was obviously a personal telephone call before identifying myself. "My name is Andrew Bell," I said. "I have a four o'clock appointment."

"Yeah? Well, just have a seat on that bench over there till you're called—and fill out this here form for me. You got a pencil, Mr. Bailey? Can't do nothin' until we have it in the files, you know?"

As soon as I completed the intake form and handed it back to this somewhat surly receptionist, who was probably annoyed for my having intruded into earshot of the intimate conversation it sounded like she was having with a would-be lover, a door to an inner office opened. Standing in the doorway with his right hand on the door knob and the left holding a coffee mug, was a tall, slightly grey and disheveled fellow wearing casual khaki pants and an attractive plaid shirt open at the neck, who at the same time looked distinguished in a subtle way hard to describe. He motioned with his head for me to enter.

By chance my case was assigned to Dr. Eugene Martin, a psychiatrist who had a private practice in suburban McLean, Virginia, and worked in the counseling center only part-time, perhaps to have some variety in his professional work. He would become a significant person in my life, although at our initial meeting I would never have guessed such a development.

Dr. Martin seemed slightly disdainful as I entered his office. With another nod he indicated I was to sit down. Then he got right to the point: "What's your problem?"

I was taken aback by his curtness and asked, "Wouldn't you like to know my name first?"

"I can read your name on the fucking file. What's your problem?"

I tried to ignore Dr. Martin's personality and told him why I was there. As usual in relating my situation, the emotions were always close to the surface and strong enough to break through at the slightest provocation. By the time I was finished, I was weeping. It was the first time I had really let go and cried since Missy left. I felt a real sense of release; it was pure catharsis. My initial reaction to Dr. Martin would begin to mellow a bit.

Our clinical relationship continued to be rocky, however, because his approach tended to be quite confrontational. It was particularly irritating to have my irrational thinking exposed and to be made aware, for example, that, while I may have *wanted* Missy to come back to me, I could have a fully satisfying life in her absence. Actually, Dr. Martin helped me to identify and abandon a number of irrational notions by his focusing the therapeutic process on the "here and now" and on my newly-discovered ability to change old patterns of thinking. He taught me to listen for irrational statements that sometimes slipped into my speech and helped me develop a more rational personal philosophy. In effect, Dr. Martin taught me how to counsel myself.

(Later when I described the details of these therapy sessions with Bubba, he said, "Dr. Martin sounds like an accomplished practitioner of RET. I use some RET techniques in my own pastoral counseling, and I'd say, given your intellect, sensitivity, and artistic temperament, RET's tailor made for you."

"Are you saying 'R-h-e-t-t' or what, and what is it?" I asked.

Bubba answered: "I'm saying 'R-E-T.' It's an acronym for rational-emotive therapy, which was developed by a fellow named Albert Ellis, who in turn received some of his inspiration from the writings of Epictetus—you know,

the Greek philosopher who held that a person does not have a problem because of what happens to that person, but rather because of what that person *thinks* about what has happened to him. This Dr. Martin of yours, I'm guessing, made you see that Missy's actual leaving you was not your problem, but rather the problem was your *perception* of her leaving as a loss from which you could not recover.")

Our counseling sessions gradually became a highpoint of my week. They were very helpful, and I looked forward to them as eagerly as I had looked forward to dates with Missy in high school or dates with Lake in college. During a large part of the rest of the week, however, I was largely in the same physical environment I had once shared with a beloved wife and cherished children. Their absence from my normal habitat made it hostile and, therefore, unhealthy. Dr. Martin recognized this and told me I needed to get away from it awhile. He said, "Bell, I want you to get your ass out of town for a month. The sooner, the better. When can you leave?"

I had a fair amount of leave time accrued, and our department's workload was under control. I knew I would not need to feel guilty about following through on Dr. Martin's advice. He wrote a letter to my director that was very effective. Without hesitation, question, or official comment, Jerry approved my request for what Dr. Martin termed an R and R (recovery and rehabilitation) package: a week of annual leave at a remarkable small monastery in the hills of Vermont, actually, a Benedictine abbey which accepted lay retreatants and whose monks celebrated their commitment to Christ with folk songs and dance; two weeks of temporary duty with the Bureau of Indian Affairs in Santa Fe, New Mexico; and two more weeks of annual leave, which I would spend in Ireland or wherever I wanted to go.

* * *

It was about a five-hour flight from Dulles International Airport to Albuquerque. That was ample time to relax and do some recreational reading as well as

some spiritual exercises taught to me by Brother Francis, a Thomas Merton-type monk I had grown very fond of during the ten days I had just spent at his abbey. (He had insisted on carrying my suitcase out to my car when it was time for me to leave, and as we stood there facing each other I said, "Brother Francis, being here has been a real blessing for me." His heartfelt reply was, "Andy, your presence was just as much a blessing for all of us. The reading you gave for our community after vespers last night was a rare treat. It left a lot of monks weepy-eyed. Drive safely now, and go with this wish: Metaphors be with you, always.")

Actually, I arrived in Albuquerque feeling refreshed and anticipating the next two weeks with guarded but nonetheless resurgent optimism. From the airport I took "The Road Runner," a small shuttle bus decorated with murals by a Navajo artist, up Interstate 25 some sixty miles to New Mexico's charming capital. In fact, I found the human-scale city of Santa Fe so completely charming, I dubbed it "Charleston of the Southwest."

The next morning I walked the five blocks from where I was staying, the Thunderbird Motel, to the campus of a unique Federal institution, B.I.A.'s Institute of American Indian Arts, to begin a unique Federal assignment: conducting a workshop in creative writing for Native Americans. I located and entered the administration building. It was nine o'clock but the dean had not arrived yet. (I soon learned that he and many other people in Santa Fe operated on what was termed "Indian Time." When I asked an Indian administrator about the concept, he explained, "You see, Mr. Bell, when you Anglo bureaucrats in the Land of Infinite Wisdom, I mean, Washington, decide to have a meeting, you schedule when it is to start and when it is to stop. When my people need to get together to discuss something, the meeting begins when everyone has arrived and it ends when everyone has had his say. This approach to administration has worked beautifully for us for thousands of years.") I took a seat in the waiting room and was reading the student newspaper when a faculty member walked in. She was disarmingly lovely and

projected a friendly aura of accessibility. I knew I would regret it later if I remained silent. So, after weighing for a moment the worst case scenario, a blotched self-introduction followed by a brush-off, I decided to risk striking up a conversation with her. Thus, I became acquainted with Pablita Luna.

Pablita said she taught contemporary as well as traditional Native American dance at the Institute. I told her I had majored in English before going to work for the Civil Rights Commission, and would be conducting a creative writing workshop at the Institute for the next two weeks. She was excited to learn of my plans and invited me to attend a program of modern dance her students were presenting in the fine arts auditorium that very evening. I told her I loved dance, had even had the immensely gratifying experience of seeing several of my poems choreographed, and would try to come see her students perform. I also invited her to sit in on one of my workshop sessions if she happened to have a free period.

Pablita was absolutely charming in a way I had never before encountered in a woman of any race, nationality, or age. She was petite, dark-featured, and nothing like Missy, about whom I still thought too much. I enjoyed the dance program that evening and was delightfully surprised to see Pablita dancing in the final piece—I guessed then she had been too modest to mention when she invited me that she would be dancing. Afterwards, I waited around the auditorium to congratulate her on the performance. She responded graciously, inviting me to come to her adobe where the troupe was having an informal party to celebrate the end of its season.

I had a nice time at the party and reciprocated by taking Pablita to Taos for dinner the following evening (although she provided our transportation in her four-wheel-drive Puma, a camp, fun vehicle that suited her active lifestyle and free spirit perfectly). On the trip back, it being too dark to see the countryside, Pablita had me say for her one after another of my poems. She then paid me a high compliment: "I can readily *see* why so many of your poems have been choreographed, Andy. The very words dance across the senses."

Getting to know Pablita made Santa Fe someplace special for me. Nevertheless, toward the end of my assignment there, I wrote Missy the following letter:

Santa Fe, April 23

Dear Missy,

Even if I were not being paid my regular salary (plus a generous per diem) these two weeks for conducting the workshop and tutoring students individually most of the afternoon, (some of whom, by the way, are quite talented—they write as they tend to speak, succinctly and with stark, simple, yet striking imagery) as well as also doing a bit of civil rights consultation at B.I.A.'s district office downtown—just being here and able to enjoy the barren beauty of New Mexico, which the natives refer to as the "Land of Enchantment," would have made taking the assignment and making the trip altogether worthwhile. But in another sense,

Putting most of the continent between
us
was as naive as thinking
the world is flat:
Two thousand miles are not enough
to soothe the pain of loving you
unrequitedly.
(And, if New Mexico won't do it,
why would the moon?)

I know now the futility of seeking peace
in a place;
(No Santa Fe can be more than respite.)
the solace I crave comes from inner
space.

And, in the desert's dry night,
beneath a billion distant stars,
I also realize
that
neither is distance between places
the key to relief.
Were it otherwise,
I might think in terms
of the light years required
to move beyond the range
of every memory
of you

If those lines a poem make, let's call it "In the Land of Disenchantment."

A week from now I shall be winging my way back to the Ould Sod. A fortnight there is just what the good doctor ordered to finish restoring my system. It should be a good trip if I can think of it in terms of going *to* something rather than fleeing *from* something or someone.

I've been corresponding with some Irish writers and expect to see them. I'm especially hoping to get to Listowel in County Kerry (in the southwest part of the island) and meet John B. Keane. You may recall I became enthralled with his plays the year we were at Trinity.

Hug Robin and Paul for me. I'm sending them separate postcards and look forward to seeing them when school is out for the summer. You did say they could spend a couple of weeks with me, didn't you?

By the way, soon you'll have completed your first year of medical school. So, how is M.U.S.C.? Still looking forward to a specialization in pediatrics? Remembering how you mothered our own two and how the other neighborhood

> children were always drawn to you, I'm betting on your success. The cost (emotionally speaking) has at times seemed excessive, but Romans 8:28 is still my motto—and who knows how much suffering will be alleviated or how many lives saved through your hands . . . .
>
> *Paz y alegría,*
> Andy

For my last evening in the Land of Enchantment, Pablita had a special surprise for me, a gesture spawned as much by her lively imagination as by her generous spirit. With this gesture Pablita would permanently endear herself to me. She prepared a picnic supper for us, picked me up at the Thunderbird Motel, where I had been getting my things together for an early flight out of Albuquerque the following morning, and drove us to a remote mesa some twenty miles southwest of Santa Fe.

There, the panoramic view was breathtaking. I have never seen a photograph or painting which captured the full scope of its splendor; such are the limitations of any two-dimensional rendering, no matter how competent, of something so vast. The endless miles of barren beauty together with the dry, mild air of late April provided an eminently poetic setting.

I was not familiar with the exotic food we ate, but it was delicious and satisfied many hungers. Her herb tea was like a nectar. While the setting was not conducive to superfluous chatter, there was, more importantly, the communion of kindred minds. As we finished eating, the sun was approaching the horizon and suddenly the whole western sky exploded with the most dazzling array of colors imaginable.

Enthralled, before I could restrain myself I was involuntarily quoting Solomon barely loud enough for Pablita to overhear: "Truly the light is sweet, and a pleasant thing it is for the eyes to behold the sun."

Recognizing the quote, Pablita said, "Yes, and one wonders if Solomon were inspired in ancient Israel by a sunset like ours when he wrote that—from Ecclesiastes,

isn't it?"

I was reimpressed with this many-faceted human being whose companionship had been so serendipitous; she went up several more notches in my esteem. "You're familiar with it!" I said more by way of delight than as a question.

"Several years ago, I went through a very difficult period. My fiancé had died in Viet Nam, and it became very difficult to concentrate on my work. It felt like the spark of creativity had gone out inside me. I came to this same spot one afternoon for solace. I had brought my Bible along, although I did not particularly feel like reading it that day. I was somewhat preoccupied by my obligation to choreograph IAIA's entry for the National Collegiate Dance Festival and I had no *earthly* idea of what to do. Anyhow, toward sunset I finally opened my Bible at random and there it was, the verse that is obviously also very special to you, Andy. As soon as I read it, I remembered a friend in Phoenix who must be one of the most talented lighting designers in the country, and in my mind I saw my dance. He and I collaborated and I don't know how it was done, but he managed to bathe the dancers, who were meant subliminally to represent a pair of mated eagles, in a slow swirl of all the colors of a desert sunset. For want of a better title, we called it 'Enchanted Sunset.'"

"And how was it received?" I asked.

"Well, it took top honors in the festival that year, but, obviously, I cannot take all the credit."

Slipping off her sandals and pulling a small cassette tape player from the bottom of the picnic basket, Pablita said, "Your poems, my friend, have made me weep, and they have made me smile. Some have opened in my heart vistas as lovely as that sunset. Your words will remain with me long after your flesh and bones are far away. Hearing you say them has been like receiving a special gift, and in return I want to teach you the essence of the dance I just told you about to help you remember this moment forever."

Then, with the stirring music of "Zorba's Dance" enveloping us, Pablita took my hands and led me in a

simple choreographic tribute to the retiring sun as a pair of eagles—I swear—circled low overhead. My spirit soared. Afterward, with my heart still pounding, I squeezed the hand of my hostess and said, "Thank you, Enchantress of the Setting Sun. I needed that."

She responded by moving close to me and saying, "I know, Man Who Weaves With Words, and I sense you need this too," loosening the long, fringed, multi-colored belt from around her waist and retying it around both of us. Thus bound together, Pablita completed this ritual of friendship by lifting herself on her toes and kissing my lips lightly but ever so sweetly, then giving me a lingering embrace as satisfying as any I have ever known. There was no suggestion of a sexual expression of this intimacy—Pablita had perceived already I was still too much in love with my estranged wife to lie with anyone else for many moons to come. That glorious moment was nonetheless memorable, and in the sunset on the inside of my eyelids, her barefooted, bronzed image will continue to dance as long as I live.

Communion

From its beginning, Bubba's ministry at St. Cecilia's was exceedingly effective even as the seeds of controversy were being sown. His sermons brought new insights to old theology. His sometimes irreverent retelling of stories from the Bible delighted most hearers and at least for a few made these stories relevant for the first time in their lives. The essence of his teaching and preaching was accessible on some meaningful level to everyone who came to hear him.

From all over the Lowcountry increasingly large numbers of people did come to hear Bubba. Many who continued to come week after week took to heart his exhortation from the pulpit, "Be joyful in your worship. You can let it all hang out before the Lord!" Membership increased significantly. Attendance at church services tripled. On most Sundays there were few seats left for latecomers, regardless of whether they were visitors, new members, or tenured pillars of the parish. On some Sundays no seats were left.

Of course, not all the lifelong members of St. Cecilia's were pleased with the influx of "outsiders" into their midst. They rued the appropriation of their ancestral pews. They were discomforted by the charismatic tendencies displayed by many of the newcomers. They were dismayed by the many hands held high during the singing of hymns and were absolutely appalled by the occasional crying out of uninhibited worshippers blessed with the gift of tongues. The disgruntled were discreet, however, and their displeasure was muted.

Overall, Bubba's relationships with the vestry as well as with the congregation-at-large were mutually satisfying. As a priest he was popular in his own parish;

moreover, as a well-connected native of a connection-conscious city, he was well known even beyond church circles. All over Charleston and the surrounding areas, he was almost as recognizable as the long-time mayor. Gradually, Bubba became something of a local celebrity.

A year passed. One morning Bubba arrived at St. Cecilia's with a subliminal sense of expectation. It was too subtle to be accounted for by his usual optimism.

Pulling into the church parking lot, he parked his white Porsche convertible in the space reserved for "Rector." After raising the top and listening to the final minute of a favorite program, "Morning Edition," on the local public radio station, he got out and walked spiritedly toward the entrance. Inside, Bubba exchanged warm greetings with the secretary, a woman about sixty who had been working at St. Cecilia's long enough to see several rectors come and go.

"Good morning glory, Gloria," he quipped.

"Good morning, Father Brinson. How are you?"

"I'm doing very well, my child, except when you call me 'Father.' Then suddenly I feel old age creep up another inch on me. As I've said before, I wish you'd call me 'Bubba.'"

"I'm sorry, Father Brinson. It's just that I've addressed all the rectors here as 'Father' so long, it's hard to change. Forgive me, I don't mean any disrespect," she said as they both laughed. Then she added, "The mail was delivered unusually early this morning. But I've already sorted it. There's quite a stack for you including a letter from the Presiding Bishop's office and one piece marked 'Personal.' Those I never open, of course. It's all on your desk. Good luck."

"Thanks, Gloria. I'm going to recommend the vestry give you a Labor Day bonus. Speaking of which, I don't want to see you here on Monday. Enjoy the long weekend. St. Cecilia's will survive somehow," he said, walking toward his study.

As soon as he entered his study Bubba adjusted the venetian blinds to let in enough morning sunlight to

make artificial lighting unnecessary. The soft sunlight and eclectic decor of the room made it a pleasant place to work. Before settling at his desk, he went to the kitchen and brought back a mug of steaming black coffee.

Looking through the stack of new mail, Bubba's attention was seized by a pastel-shaded envelope on the bottom. It was the one marked "Personal." The artistic handwriting was very familiar. There was no return address, although the Washington, D.C., postmark assured him it was from Priscilla. She wrote:

August 30, 1988

Dear Bubba,

I'm as surprised to be writing this as you will be to receive it. Please at least peruse it before you allow yourself to react.

In a few weeks, September 21-22 to be exact, I expect to pass through Charleston. I'll be driving by myself. Margo, my sister in Daytona Beach, has asked me to come down that week while she's having some surgery—minor, but she'll need help with Kelly and Tara, my cute little six- and four-year-old nieces. They're precocious and quite lively. Yes, they take after their Aunt Pris!

Since I've never been in your holy city (or is it "Holy City"?), I plan to stay overnight and take in some of its reputed charm whether you care to see me or not. I hope that by now and under these circumstances you'd be comfortable meeting for a cup of coffee or a nonthreatening walk along the beautiful Battery you used to tell me about.

I am trying to get on with my life as you seem to have done with yours—and, commendably, to have done with such aplomb and enviable grace. It would help me to do that too, if I could see you, say good-bye to you face to face. Doesn't a relationship which was once so sweet deserve the consideration of proper closure?

You once gave me a small poem poster, which graced the front of my refrigerator for years. On a background of light blue like the cloudless Carolina sky which favored us the time we visited the Outer Banks (loving and lingering on Ocracoke long enough to miss the ferry back to Hatteras), two seagulls, one slightly larger than the other, are shown in perfectly parallel flight. The pairing could represent a relationship between a man and woman, free spirited and in love. The poem was "Moment," by your friend Andrew Bell.

Many times I have been struck by the irony of its relevance to us, wondered if somehow we were Andrew's inspiration. Do you remember it? I do—

Like two young gulls
from different flocks,
flying solo and afraid
to adventure too far
over uncharted seas,
the trajectories of our lives
met only once,
were parallel
in a narrow moment of sunlight
before diverging
to opposite infinities

Bubba, I do hope you'll let us have just one more moment of sunlight, moonlight, or whatever is convenient. I know you'll let me know, so I look forward to your reply.

Sincerely,
Priscilla

Bubba glanced at his appointments calendar. September 21 would be a Wednesday. The church's usual mid-week Communion service would be at five o'clock that afternoon. It would not be inappropriate, he thought, to invite her to the service and to have dinner at a nice nearby restaurant afterwards.

"That should be safe," he said to himself, "since she says she's only staying overnight, and anything less would be unthinkably inhospitable. After all, this is Charleston, not New York City."

Bubba took a sheet of St. Cecilia letterhead and wrote a reply immediately. He addressed the envelope to the post office box Priscilla had used in the past for their confidential correspondence. In the absence of her giving any other address, he correctly assumed she had retained that box. Just before sealing the envelope, however, it occurred to him that using church stationery was not prudent. He rewrote his response on plain sheets of paper.

September 2, 1988

Dear Pris,

You're right. I am surprised, but pleasantly. Last December I almost sent you a Christmas card, which is still here in my desk. It's a UNICEF card with a stylized rendition of the Nativity in earthy shades of brown, gray and white by a Ugandan artist. It reminds me of some of your own more realistic work (as contrasted with your abstracts which I always had trouble relating to). The printed greeting inside in five languages says what I hoped our parting would ensure for everyone: *Peace on Earth/Paix sur la Terre/Paz en la Tierra/* etc. Why didn't I send it? I don't know. Perhaps I wanted to say something more and couldn't. Anyhow, it would be good to see you in Charleston on the 21st. There should be

some solace in such a reunion for both of us.

Please know, Pris, that letting go of you was the hardest thing I ever had to do. But I think it was also one of the few truly noble things I've ever done. At the moment of truth, images of your boys coming home from school day after day, year after year, with no mom to welcome them with hugs and milk and chocolate chip cookies—it was a bigger brick than I could fit into the already bulging sack of guilt I carry on my back through life. (Of course, that rarely happened because the artist spent so much time working in her studio.)

I wasn't too concerned about Harry. The unfaithful bastard deserved, in some sense, whatever you decided to do. But the boys were innocent bystanders, unaware child actors in a tragedy being written and directed by adults. Steve, Randy, and Bobby didn't deserve losing you—and I'm still certain that Harry would've won permanent custody had you run away with me to San Francisco. Having me would never have compensated you for so great a loss, and, ultimately, it would have embittered you.

Often I meditate on this from the standpoint of ethics: Can one still get credit for a good deed (like my letting go of you) even if one sometimes regrets it afterwards?

We celebrate Holy Communion at St. Cecilia's on Wednesday afternoons at 5. I'll be free by 6:30. Why don't you plan to attend H.C., and we can go out to dinner right afterwards.

Fondly,
B.

Priscilla called Bubba at the church Wednesday morning. Bubba recognized an old pleasure in hearing her voice on the phone. He asked, "Did you just arrive in town?"

"No. Actually, I arrived about eleven last night, which I felt was too late to call. So I checked into a charming bed and breakfast place on East Bay Street an artist friend had recommended. I thought I'd take a bus tour, which leaves from the new Visitor's Center at ten. I believe it's called 'Doing the Charleston.' I could meet you when you're free—at six-thirty, didn't you say?"

"The bus tour sounds good—I know the fellows who run it. But aren't you coming to hear me preach? You don't get to hear a sermon like mine very often, you know."

Priscilla was reluctant to commit herself. She said, "That's too true, Bubba. But as much as I know I'd enjoy the service and hearing you speak, I—I just feel it wouldn't be right. I may not be an active member of one anymore, but I have a deep respect for churches. I don't want to be guilty of any sort of sacrilege."

"That's pretty heavy, Pris."

"Am I overstating what I mean? How about 'hypocrisy'—better word? Couldn't I just wait for you somewhere?"

"You're too good to be true, Pris. If you really feel you're a sinner, you'd be among kindred souls. If everyone were perfect, there would be no need for my profession. And a person's whole life need not have been lived flawlessly in order to qualify as one of the 'pure in heart.' It would mean a lot to me to look out and see you in the congregation today—and to serve you communion."

"Well, couldn't we just leave it open? If I'm feeling brave—or should I say 'brazen'—this afternoon, I'll come," Priscilla said, ending on a note of nervous laughter.

As a rule, Bubba's mid-week service sermons were short. His homily that day to the congregation that included his former lover, an accomplice in adultery, would be no exception. He had been doing a series on the Beatitudes and, while working in his study in

mid-afternoon, succumbed to an impulse to rearrange the schedule so as to speak that day on Jesus' assertion, "Blessed *are* the pure in heart; for they shall see God."

But at the last minute, Bubba changed his mind again and began his homily by reading a passage from the Gospel of John. Not surprisingly, it was the story about the scribes and Pharisees bringing before Jesus a woman who had been caught in the act of adultery. Bubba said: "I can imagine that she was young, had soft brown hair and hazel eyes, and was very pretty. More frightened than embarrassed, but still somewhat defiant. According to the apostle, the scribes and Pharisees reminded Jesus that Moses' law demanded that the adulteress be stoned to death and, trying to trap Jesus into saying something which could be used against Him later, asked His own opinion.

"Jesus, of course, although He acted as if He hadn't heard them, was no dummy. He stooped down and with His finger doodled on the ground. The Scriptures do not record what He was drawing. It may have been Stars of David. Jesus was a Jew, as you well know. Or, inasmuch as He'd been trained as a carpenter, it may've been a design for something He had wanted to build but never got around to doing before beginning His ministry. Now that would be readily understandable because many of us with very worthy goals have experienced never getting *'a round to-it'* and doodle away the years of our lives in pursuit of—of what, pray tell me."

"To keep them guessing, Jesus' doodle may have been an abstract—not unlike something in that controversial exhibition currently at the Gibbes. What's important is that his momentary silence focused the gathered crowd's attention on what happened next.

"When the woman's accusers insisted on an answer, Jesus stood and said something like, 'O.K., but let him who is without sin among you cast the first stone at her,' then He stooped down to doodle some more. St. John says that, at that point, the scribes and Pharisees, (who, I think, epitomized a kind of hypocrisy even some of us Episcopalians are subject to) 'being convicted by their own conscience,' slipped away—like Lowcountry grass

snakes, I suppose.

"Jesus and the woman—Shall we give her a name? No, John had the discretion not to identify her, so neither should we—Jesus and the woman were left standing in front of the crowd. Jesus asked her where were her accusers and, rhetorically, if not even one of them had condemned her. She answered, 'No, my Lord,' probably with a mixture of meekness, relief, and gratitude. Jesus said, 'Well, neither do I,' and then, like the universal 'Be Good' injunction we parents give our children—which even the extraterrestrial gave the little girl in that delightful 'E.T.' film—He said 'Go and sin no more.'"

Bubba was looking at Priscilla as he finished. The upbeat conclusion of his homily had left her and most of the others in the congregation with smiles on their faces and feelings of edification within their hearts.

At the invitation during the celebration of Holy Communion, Priscilla started to rise, then caught herself. After vacillating all afternoon, at that moment of truth her sense of propriety checked her impetuosity. Bubba had not really anticipated that she would partake of the sacrament and was only mildly disappointed.

By the time Bubba had served the last communicant and covered the chalice, he was very eager to commence the visit with Priscilla. Even so, his sense of priestly responsibility did not allow him to succumb to the temptation to use the short form of the blessing. The people were used to the long form.

The fair-haired shepherd stood at the center of the altar rail and raised his hand over his flock. Then, in a voice which epitomized pastoral tenderness, he pronounced the blessing, using the traditional long form: "The peace of God, which passeth all understanding, keep your hearts and minds in the knowledge and love of God, and of his Son Jesus Christ our Lord; and the blessing of God Almighty, the Father, the Son, and the Holy Ghost, be amongst you, and remain with you, and all whom you love, always." (The words at the end, "and all whom you love," are not to be found in The Book of Common Prayer, but they suited Bubba's temperament, and no one ever challenged him on his use of them.)

Everyone, even Priscilla, joined the priest then in saying "Amen."

Dinner

Priscilla was pretty that afternoon. A sleeveless white dress worn with a colorful sash around the waist complemented her lightly tanned limbs and a figure any woman could be proud of, a figure which belied the fact that she was an almost middle-aged mother of three. A ribbon matching the magenta sash pulled thick auburn hair back from her healthy face far enough to expose large gold earrings, a token of Bubba's affection years earlier. The shade of her full lips and manicured nails complemented that of the sash and the ribbon. An overall subtle effect of mystery, artistry, desirability, was enhanced by the absence of any rings, wedding or otherwise, which could only have compromised the perfection of her slender fingers.

After the service she had walked outside to look around the church grounds and wait for Bubba. By the time the personable priest had finished greeting everyone who wished to speak with him, Priscilla was in the graveyard trying to read the weathered inscriptions on old tombstones.

Reading epitaphs is a ready way to supplement one's classroom-acquired knowledge of the South Carolina Lowcountry's early history, particularly the domestic details of that history, and Priscilla found them interesting. She took quiet pride in being a perpetual student. This love for learning was among the qualities that had made the ill-advised relationship with her so irresistible to Bubba.

The priest was still in his cassock and still smiling when he walked up silently behind her. Before speaking, he hesitated a moment to admire her classy appearance. Knowing her had occasioned some of the sweetest

moments of his life. He remembered now how much he had missed her after ending their affair.

He asked, "Can I entice you away from the dead with the promise of some of Charleston's famous cuisine?"

Priscilla was already returning the smile as she turned toward him and said, "Your sermon provided a great deal of food for thought—Shall I say a veritable feast for the spirit? It really was wonderful, Bubba, and uplifting as well. I'm glad you urged me to come today. But, as you yourself always said, the body needs nourishing too. And I do have that long drive to Daytona tomorrow. Let's!"

"Fine," Bubba said. "Let me just go over to the sacristy long enough to change into my civies. It would not be seemly, my Lady, for someone so classy to be accompanied by a bozo wearing a backward collar."

"You jest," she reassured him, "clerical collars become you."

"Be right back," he said, already heading for the sacristy.

Ten minutes later Bubba and Priscilla were walking toward Tommy Condon's, an Irish pub and restaurant on Church Street and his favorite watering hole, to decide over drinks where to have dinner. It was a pleasant walk of about five blocks. First they headed north on Meeting Street. They passed old houses, a number of which were adorned with plaques awarded by the Preservation Society of Charleston, stately-columned South Carolina Society Hall, St. Michael's Episcopal Church, the Federal Court House and Post Office, Charleston County Courthouse, City Hall and behind it Washington Park, and a side street named Chalmers paved with cobblestones which had served as ballast in colonial sailing ships. Here they were in front of an imposing building, which brought to mind the Greek temples of antiquity.

Bubba said, "This hall is headquarters for the Hibernian Society. I believe it was built in 1840 and the style Greek Revival with that imposing portico and these wrought iron gates. Besides the Irish harp adorning the gate here, note the gold one on the green background

above the entrance door. Isn't that just stunning, Pris? When I party on St. Patrick's Day, I wear a tie with an identical motif, gold harps on green background."

Priscilla laughingly said, "Well, I see you're as proud as ever of your Irish ancestry. Some things never change, do they?"

Bubba answered, "Well, even if we Brinsons are more American now than Irish, I can't help but be inspired every time I walk by here. Those harps remind me of an ancient heritage no one can ever take away, a heritage of freedom and faith that's even older than the institutional Church."

After describing Hibernian Hall, Bubba added, "This is also where one of the South's most famous or, at least, most exclusive social events is held, the St. Cecilia Ball I've told you about that's sponsored by the St. Cecilia Society. My church and the society share Cecilia's name, but nothing else. There's no official or historical connection between the two. And my family has never been involved with the Society or its ball either. It never bothered me, but I remember once my sister Missy earnestly asking our father how she could get an invitation to the ball. He hugged her and laughed and explained that, because we didn't live here on the peninsula, the most elite part of Charleston even if not the oldest, she would be persona non grata at the ball. He also told her that the Brinsons had arrived in South Carolina too late to qualify. They didn't come over from Ireland, from County Monaghan, to be exact, until 1760 and Charleston society was almost a century old by then! Dad teased that she should be grateful Ashley Hall was willing to enroll her, what with her paternal Irish ancestry and red hair."

Priscilla asked, "Do you mean the Ashley Hall School that Vice President Bush's wife, Barbara, attended?"

"The same. And after Mrs. Bush became the Second Lady of the Land, or, should I say, the Vice Lady, Missy joked she had sat at the same desk in history class that Barbara had used, not to mention another seat somewhere else."

They continued talking, crossed Queen Street, and

came to the Gibbes Museum of Art, pausing long enough to read a poster announcing the current exhibition which Bubba had referred to earlier in his sermon. Walking on, Priscilla mused aloud, "Perhaps I should apply for an exhibition here. What do you think of the idea?"

"Why not? I think they want to be well rounded—you know, to get exhibitionists from all parts of the country," Bubba quipped.

They passed the aptly named Circular Congregational Church, and at the corner this handsome couple turned right on Cumberland Street, pausing again at the Powder Magazine. Here Bubba remarked in his typical irreverent manner, "The Lords Proprietors, Anthony Ashley Cooper, Sir Bill Berkeley, who was the Earl of Craven, really, Johnny Colleton, and all that crew, had this quaint structure built about 1713 to store gunpowder. Ostensibly, the gunpowder was to be used in case of an attack by Indians insane enough or ungrateful enough to try to recover their ancient homelands, or in case of an attack by evangelical Spaniards from Florida seeking to spread Catholicism, not only among the heathen, but also among the heretics of Henry's Church."

"I assume you refer to Henry VIII," Priscilla said.

"Yes, that same half-sane, backsliding, egotistical 'Defender of the Faith.' May his soul rest in purgatory and the souls of all six of his wives rest in peace. Anyhow, I think the good Lords Proprietors really wanted to have it on hand to keep the colonists in line. The way English nobility stuck it to the poor colonists it's amazing we didn't have the Revolution almost a century sooner, isn't it? In any case, some would say Charleston's been one kind of powder keg or another ever since."

Then the two turned left on Church Street and were at Tommy Condon's. After they took a table outside on the pub's porch, Bubba asked, "What would quench your thirst, my gracious guest?"

Priscilla laughed, "I put myself at your mercy, O noble host. Just as long as it's not Scotch, which I still like as much as I like castor oil, I'm easy, as you know."

Bubba laughed too, "Don't worry, this is a good Irish

pub. Tommy probably doesn't even serve it here. May I suggest what I'm having, an Irish whiskey on the rocks?"

"Will it taste anything like Scotch?"

"Not at all. Irish is a smooth, sipping whiskey and more like an excellent sour mash bourbon—Rebel Yell, for example, or Jack Daniel's—than anything else, although its flavor is as unique as a unicorn. Do you remember my friend Andy Bell—he was also my brother-in-law. Of course, you do. Well, Andy introduced me to Irish whiskey after he and my sister Missy came home from their year at Trinity College. It was love at first sip. You know, it's a pity so many Americans think it's only good for Irish coffee or to be drunk only on St. Patrick's Day."

"Well, if it's as 'unique as a unicorn,' I'd better try it. Bubba, you can still talk me into anything. Did you ever kiss the Blarney Stone?"

"I believe it's the other way around, Pris. As for the stone, I guess you could say I've kissed it by proxy. Missy and Andy were there, bent over backwards out of a castle tower, they tell me, to reach it. I gave my little sister a 'welcome home' kiss when they returned to the States."

The waitress appeared. She happened to be new and a charming colleen. Some dialectal repartee between her and Bubba revealed her name to be "Nuala." She was from "Yeats Country," or County Sligo. The dark-haired young woman then took their order inside to the bar and returned quickly with their drinks.

Bubba raised his glass to Priscilla's, looked deeply into her eyes, and toasted her: "*Saoghal agus Sonas agus Sláinte,* as they say on the ould sod."

After another of her infectious laughs, Priscilla took a sip of her drink and said, "Bubba this *is* good, but what am I drinking to?"

"My Gaelic is a bit rusty, but I think it means 'Life and Happiness and Health,' though not necessarily in that order. Let it mean what you will, Pris."

"That's risky, but if you insist—anyhow, I like it. Do you know any others?"

Bubba clinked his glass with hers again and said loftily: "*Córas Iompair ʹEireann.*"

"That sounds grand, Bubba. What does it mean?"

Bubba chuckled. "Well, loosely translated, it means 'National Transportation System of Ireland.' If you're ever lucky enough to go there, you'll see a logo with the initials 'C.I.E.' on the sides of buses and trains."

With the Irish Tri-color flapping beside the American flag above the porch where they relaxed, Bubba told Priscilla about his former brother-in-law and lifelong friend's contact with the I.R.A. during his and Missy's year at Trinity College in Dublin. Bubba related how Missy had been very enthusiastic about studying Anglo-Irish literature and living in the seaside village of Dalkey about twelve miles south of Dublin for a whole year. At first, it seemed like an idyllic existence. She became very fearful, however, when she accidently learned her husband was about to become involved in I.R.A. espionage activity. Missy had then given Andy an ultimatum: He had to promise her he'd cease all contact with the I.R.A. immediately or she would return home with their baby daughter Robin on the next flight. Andy acquiesced, albeit with a heavy heart. Andy had been outraged by the resumption of violence in Northern Ireland, which he attributed primarily to British insensitivity and Victorian vestiges of an imperial mentality.

Bubba and Priscilla agreed that the continued British occupation of Northern Ireland was an anachronism in an era which was seeing freedom make such significant strides all across Europe. "And isn't it strange," Priscilla remarked, "that as a nation which owes so much to the Irish for our own independence we've done so little to help them in return."

Bubba acknowledged this anomaly of American foreign policy and mentioned the irony of Hibernian Hall being used for a huge dinner honoring Prince Charles during a recent visit to Charleston. "'Tis a shame, to be sure, me lass, that the limey lobby in this country's so bloody strong. Shocking!"

Priscilla winced at the harsh truth of what Bubba said and smiled almost simultaneously at the Irish idiom he used. Her own reading tended to confirm what Andy

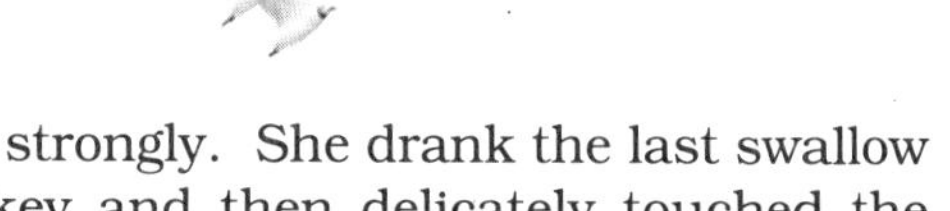

and Bubba felt so strongly. She drank the last swallow of her Irish whiskey and then delicately touched the green napkin to her lips.

Bubba glanced at his watch and said, "We should decide soon about dinner. We could have some delicious corned beef and cabbage here, which I try to come in for at least once a month, or some hearty Irish stew, which would be just fine now and absolutely perfect on a cold winter night, or—I have an idea. Let me just go make a quick call."

Bubba went to a phone booth, looked up the number, and called another of his favorite restaurants, Robert's of Charleston. He was smiling when he returned and said, "We're in luck—there had just been a cancellation. A candlelit table for two will be awaiting us at a place you'll want to write home about."

Most places on the lower part of the peninsula are located no more than a few blocks from wherever one happens to be. Robert's was no exception. A five-minute walk through the colorful old City Market had the two hungry diners at its door.

The hostess recognized Bubba, greeting him warmly, "Father Brinson, it's so nice to see you again—and to have your guest. Your table is ready. If you'll just follow me . . . ."

Even before they reached their table, Priscilla was taken by the ambiance of the place, its hunter's green and deep coral decor, the soft light and linens, as well as the sparkling crystal, attractive dinnerware, and real flowers on each table. The restaurant's unique format provided for one seating a night and could accommodate sixty people. It appeared to be at capacity. The chef and owner, Robert Dickson, sang Broadway show tunes and arias from various operas between courses. His restaurant and he himself were so popular among locals as well as tourists that no one was bothered by his having been born in New Jersey!

Almost as soon as Bubba and Priscilla were seated, they were each served a thick slice of warm scallop mousse with Maine lobster sauce. A basket of freshly baked French bread and butter came about the same

time. Before starting to eat, however, the priest suggested they say grace. He held her hand gently under the table and discreetly thanked the Lord for what they were about to receive. With the first bite, Priscilla sensed she had begun a memorable meal. "Bubba, I didn't know anything from the sea could be *this* tasty!"

As the tables were cleared, the singing chef held their attention with a romantic piece from Bernstein's *West Side Story*. Priscilla approved, "Bubba, I love it!"

Then a colorful salad was served, followed by a selection from an Italian opera. The next course was roast breast of duckling, sensually sauced with a touch of garlic, raspberry puree, and some exotic Oriental seasonings. A fine white wine, one of several served during the evening, was brought with the duckling.

Bubba, noting the fowl was from North Carolina, said, "That reference in your note to the Outer Banks brought back warm memories. Do you remember the day we were driving up to see the lighthouse on the northern end of the Banks, near Corolla? You were looking toward the water, mesmerized, I suppose, by the sea oats and sea gulls. I yelled 'DUCK!' You were startled, then amused as I pointed out to you the sign indicating we were entering the community by that name."

Priscilla laughed, "I remember not being amused immediately, but I did come around later—and tried to pull it on you on our way back to Nag's Head."

After the duckling, a dollop of fresh fruit sorbet was brought to refresh their palates and Robert sang another aria. The main entree was next, center-cut tenderloin of Angus beef, grilled and enhanced by a sauce flavored with wine and brandy, and accompanied by fresh vegetables.

Bubba asked Priscilla about her art, "Are you painting much these days? I treasure the three paintings you gave me—your self-portrait most of all. The pose is precious. With your arms crossed and holding the paint brush to your chin—it catches the essence, I think, of your creative psyche."

"I'm glad you still like it, Bubba, and yes, I'm pleased to say the past two years have been very productive. It

took a while to get over losing you—I did almost nothing for a full year—but, I'm scheduled for a show at a new gallery in Georgetown, Washington's Georgetown, next spring. It takes six months to a year to get ready for these shows."

"I won't promise to come, but send me an invitation anyhow," Bubba said. He was pensive for a moment and added, "Priscilla, Priscilla, there was no other way. I hurt, too—for a long time; but innocent others were about to be hurt at least as deeply . . . ."

At that moment Robert came out to the dining room and his patrons hushed themselves in anticipation of his next number. He then announced: "Ladies and gentlemen, as we begin serving your dessert and coffee, I'd like to sing for you two final pieces, both from a Broadway hit of about twenty years ago, *Man of La Mancha*. They are 'To Each His Dulcinea' and 'The Impossible Dream.' And, as a special treat for all of us, I'm going to ask one of our guests here tonight, a very talented pianist as well as painter from Washington, D.C., to accompany me. This may come as a surprise to her, but, Ms. Priscilla Browne, would you come join me, please."

Robert held out his hand toward Priscilla to beckon her as the other guests turned to see who the special treat would be—as well as who she was with. Priscilla, surprised, but possessing too much poise and self-confidence to be either annoyed or embarrassed by Bubba's apparently advance arrangement with Robert, turned to her host, forced a frown, and said with mock disgust, "Bubba Brinson, I might have known you would make me play for my supper!"

"Well, I just don't know what came over me," Bubba responded with equally mock contrition. Then with his impish grin, he added, "But go for it, Pris. Robert's waiting, as we all are."

Priscilla played flawlessly; Robert sang as if the songs had been written with his voice in the composer's mind. Their joint effort was a hit with the gathered guests, who greeted the opening with brief but warm applause and afterwards gave the pair a prolonged ovation.

Priscilla returned to her table glowing; Bubba was beaming. "Pris, y'all were wonderful. I'm truly proud of you." Their mood had become as sweet as the chocolate raspberry torte they relished then with freshly brewed coffee—and the solace of being together.

On the sidewalk, Priscilla put her arm through Bubba's and praised the dinner again. "I've never had a more delightful meal, Bubba—and I'm *happy* being with you tonight."

The moon had risen. It was only four days from being full, and in the soft lunar light St. Cecilia's steeple stood out against the cloudless sky, its slender spire directing their reverent gaze toward countless stars.

"Bubba, Charleston is just—just heavenly at night. Look at your steeple! I wish I could see the view from the top. Could we go up there just for a quick look?"

Something deep inside Bubba made him hesitate for a second, but no rational reason not to grant her request articulated itself.

"Sure, why not?" Bubba answered. "The steeple does need some repairs and wouldn't withstand the full force of a major hurricane, but it shouldn't topple under the weight of just two people. We'll need a key from the church office. Come on."

Bubba had Priscilla precede him on the narrow, winding stairs so that he could catch her if she slipped. At Bubba's suggestion she had removed her shoes to make climbing easier. Her smooth legs were bare as always in warm weather. Ascending the stairs, Priscilla's heels were at Bubba's eyelevel. By the light of his flashlight, he saw that her ankles were still as perfect as he had remembered them.

Coming out onto an open platform just below the spire, Bubba announced, "This is as far as we can go while we're still alive."

A little winded, Priscilla said, "Oh my! Bubba, this is even better than I expected."

"Only true modesty kept me from telling you earlier that it's the best view in town."

She laughed and said, "Well, I'm glad to know you've held on to all your virtues, including that one."

Bubba proceeded to point out places of interest: "Over there—the steeple that's almost as tall as ours—that's St. Philip's Episcopal Church. John C. Calhoun was buried in their graveyard, although he was neither a Charlestonian nor an Episcopalian. In fact, I've heard he helped to establish a Unitarian church in Washington, maybe the one you used to attend occasionally. The next steeple to the right of St. Philip's is St. Michael's. They and St. Cecilia's are the three oldest Episcopal churches on the peninsula and, I guess, there's some competition among us, although we never officially acknowledge it.

"Speaking of churches, I'm sorry we can't see St. Stephen's from here. It's in that direction, but all those new hotels and bank buildings block the view. I'm as enthusiastic about St. Stephen's as I am about my own church. It's the only truly racially integrated Episcopal congregation in the city. If I could get our vestry to allocate the same proportion of St. Cecilia's budget as St. Stephen's does of its own to meeting the immediate needs of the community, the city's shelters for the homeless could be converted to other uses and all the hungry would be well-fed. Unfortunately, my flock doesn't grasp what Jesus had in mind when he said, 'For you have the poor always with you . . . .' Even Kurt Vonnegut in his book *Palm Sunday* argues that Jesus was only joking when He said that. Anyhow, St. Stephen's vicar has been sort of my mentor since I returned to Charleston. Did your tour bus go by there today?"

"Yes, and the bus stopped so the tourists could get out and take pictures. As you know, I don't carry cameras, but I got out, too, for a closer look and found the front door slightly ajar. I stepped inside and had a strong sense of peacefulness, of something there seems to be relatively less of in larger churches."

"I know precisely what you mean, Pris, and I agree. Anyhow, the long straight street running beside St. Michael's is Broad, Broad Street, I mean. At that end is the Exchange Building, where George Washington was entertained and human beings were bought and sold. I'm not implying that he was entertained by the slave trade even if he owned some. I assume that's why it's called the

'Exchange Building.' Opposite St. Michael's is the post office and Federal Court House and on the other corners the County Court House and City Hall—Corner of Four Laws the collection is called. You were probably in all those places on your tour today and I'm boring you with the repetition."

Turning around, he pointed and said, "That's the Ashley River at the other end of Broad. I grew up on the other side. Our house was on the west bank, which is not to be confused with the West Bank we loved in Paris."

Priscilla slipped in softly, "Or you could say 'the one on which we loved in Paris.'"

Bubba did not know how to respond to that bit of intimate nostalgia, except by continuing his commentary. "Our house was exactly across the river from The Citadel, which you can see over there."

Turning again, he pointed toward the harbor. "There, about midway between the Sullivan's Island Lighthouse and the east end of James Island, you can see the outline of Fort Sumter, that quintessential symbol of Southern unrepentance."

Priscilla was standing close to Bubba, her bare arm against the sleeve of his blue blazer. Her soft, curly brown hair occasionally brushed his face as he leaned close to point out to her some landmark on the dark horizon. The hair's clean, faintly sweet scent was intoxicating, inciting memories of seeing it spread around her sleeping head on beds they had shared . . . .

Priscilla listened to Bubba's commentary with rapt attention, it seemed, awaiting the moment, as if it were spontaneous, to exclaim: "Oh, Bubba, this is beautiful! I've never seen a city so—so enchanting. Thank you," she said, cupping his cheeks in her hands and giving him a quick kiss of gratitude.

By impulse, Bubba's hands went to her waist. They looked into each other's eyes with a hunger which had not been satisfied at dinner. He pulled Priscilla to him and their lips met in moonlight barely bright enough to see that hers were moist and slightly parted, a perennial sign of her readiness to receive him. It was a long kiss, long enough to awaken all the passion they had ever felt for

each other—in Washington, in Paris, and on the Outer Banks of North Carolina in seasons past, and, at last, on this seductive September night in the heart of Charleston.

Coming up for air, Bubba said, "I just realized—you're wearing *Fracas*, aren't you?"

"Yes. It occurred to me that the Irishman in you might appreciate a bit of a 'fracas' with an old friend on a night like this."

Uncharacteristically nonplused, Bubba could only say, "Well, anyhow, Pris, if we don't stop now, this steeple is liable to topple over."

Priscilla responded to Bubba's caution by sticking her tongue into his ear. As he nuzzled her neck, Priscilla's unique moan rose slowly, sweetly, and acted like a flammable fuel poured on the hot coals of a man's desire.

Together they sank below the level of the parapet, out of sight of their angels, and were alone—alone with themselves and their demons . . . .

As they walked back to her inn, Priscilla said, "Bubba, about that steeple, even if it had toppled over, aside from the embarrassment of creating a scene, that would have been an exciting way to go, wouldn't it?"

Bubba answered, "What can I say? It was the last night of summer. Tomorrow is not only another day, but also another season. It was like 'a space of timelessness/ in the anachronous marsh—'"

"'—of Edisto Island,'" Priscilla filled in.

"You know all Andy's poems, don't you?" Bubba asked.

"Well, I guess I know my favorites, like 'Edisto Hours.' I love its last stanza:

That brief eternity
let you look beyond yourselves
and there you found
the moments you sought . . .
just in time.

Nunc Dimittis

The storm may have started innocuously as a low, that is, simply as a weather system of depressed barometric pressure. On any given day, such weather systems spawn themselves randomly all over the face of the earth. This particular low apparently began over the eastern edge of the Atlantic or West Africa. Perhaps in the beginning it brought some benign breeze to the outskirts of the Sahara. In a week or so it was over the high seas, no longer benign, but slowly drifting westward and growing wild.

Interestingly, the hurricane this storm would become was accurately predicted three months previously. The predictor was an expert in astrometeorology, which considers planetary and solar movements in making long-range weather forecasts. Her approach, no doubt, was too unconventional for most people and, accordingly, her prediction was not widely reported.

When the winds of the storm reached requisite velocity, government policy required personification, a handle. "Hugo" was the arbitrary choice. Obviously, Hugo was the eighth tropical storm of the season. In a year mandating a feminine name for the eighth storm, it just as readily could have been called Helen or Hillary.

The list of landfalls by Hugo sounds something like a Caribbean cruise itinerary: Guadeloupe, Montserrat, Antigua, St. Kitts, the U.S. Virgin Islands, Puerto Rico. On the weather map, a line drawn through these landfalls pointed straight toward the South Carolina coast. Indeed, many of the faithful would be convinced that God viewed Charleston as a contemporary Sodom, and this time He was using a hurricane rather than fire from

Heaven to display His divine displeasure.

* * *

Tens of thousands of Lowcountry residents heeded the official calls to evacuate low-lying areas. A massive traffic jam ensued on all highways leading inland. To some refugees old enough to remember the Second World War on the home front, its anxieties and inconveniences, the situation brought back memories of blackouts, air raid sirens, half-moon headlights, the funny little stamps you had to trade for shoes and sugar, years of family outings without fathers. To others who had left the Lowcountry to serve in places like Bataan, Saipan, North Africa, Anzio, Leyte Gulf, Normandy, it triggered memories of long absences from waiting wives and growing children, forced marches, internment, the death and dismemberment of cherished comrades, wounds both physical and emotional.

To almost all the refugees pushed from their promised land by the threat of raging winds and rising waters, this mass exodus unleashed a flood of memories about the place itself, not only their respective places of residence, repose, recreation, but also the collective place, the South Carolina Lowcountry, which they worried would not be the same place upon their return.

Bubba had decided to ride out the storm in his study at the church. Notwithstanding the mayor's order for everyone to evacuate the city, Bubba felt a higher authority had called him to St. Cecilia's originally and, now, to remain at his assigned post, come hell or high water. Besides, he knew the God worshipped at St. Cecilia's was also the God of Nature.

Although church staff and volunteers had prepared all parish property for the predicted "Hurricane of the Century" as well as they knew how, Bubba still felt there could be a damage control role for someone to play. And, in view of the mayor's evacuation directive, he could not in good conscience either ask or authorize anyone other than himself to shoulder that responsibility. Despite the pleas of the senior warden, Frank Stuckey, and others who wanted him to take refuge with them on higher ground inland, he was resolute.

Frank and Bubba had first become good friends when the two were undergraduates at Sewanee and brothers in Kappa Sigma Fraternity. Frank was two years ahead of Bubba and addressed him with the compassion as well as the candidness of an older sibling. "Bubba, no one doubts your commitment to the parish and your attachment to these old buildings. I know you love St. Cecilia's as much as anybody. But I can't believe the Lord would have you be a martyr for stone and mortar; dying for a steeple is not the same as dying for people, for God's sake!"

"Frank, it's right that you and the others leave; y'all have done all anyone could ask. And I'm deeply touched by your concern for my personal safety, but I'll be all right. I feel I need to be here. I'm sure this is right for me. Go on now. I'm sure we'll be in touch soon. Go on. Let me stay and pray."

"Bubba, sometimes I think you're either a blessed idiot or a jinxed saint. I'm going now, just wish you were coming with us. God bless."

"*Nunc dimittis*, Frank."

The two men put their hands on each other's shoulders and looked into each other's eyes. The senior warden said the opening words of that canticle which begins, "Lord, now lettest thou thy servant depart in peace, according to thy word."

And Bubba, the priest, his eyes misting, responded, "For mine eyes have seen thy salvation."

"Which thou hast prepared before the face of all people," Frank added.

"To be a light to lighten the Gentiles, and to be the glory of thy people Israel," Bubba concluded.

Without another word, for any other utterance would have been superfluous, the men dropped their arms, and the senior warden turned and went out, leaving the priest alone.

The windows in his corner study, both the east window looking out on Meeting Street as well as the south window overlooking the graveyard, were shuttered on the

outside. Inside, each pane was reinforced with masking tape in the shape of St. Andrew's cross. Battery lanterns were backed up by a large supply of altar candles. There was sufficient food and bottled water for a week. A portable radio provided constant updates from Charleston-area stations. Then, after all these went silent, either when staffs were forced by rising waters to abandon studios or when transmitting towers were toppled by the equivalent of a twenty-mile wide tornado, Bubba found solace in listening to a Savannah station.

The sustained winds of 140 miles per hour sounded like the roar of an endless freight train moving along Meeting Street right outside his shuttered window. It was an eerie sound, not essentially evil but more like the pure wrath of an outraged god. When it seemed impossible that the wind could howl any louder and Bubba was feeling relief that the fabric of the church would not tear, one of the 175 miles per hour gusts confronted St. Cecilia's and there was a thundering sound similar to the sonic boom of a jet plane breaking the sound barrier. Then there was the steady deafening roar of the wind again.

With an Air Force base located in North Charleston, Bubba, like other area residents, had heard sonic booms often enough to be familiar with them, but this did not occur to him now. He felt smitten by someone he could not see. And he knew with his sixth sense the steeple lay in the street. His heart beat heavily. In the dim light of lanterns, his anguished gaze fell on the small framed photograph of Priscilla he kept on a shelf in his bookcase. Memories of their lovemaking at home in her absent husband's bed, in an oceanfront hotel with window open at Nag's Head, in Parisian pensions, in St. Cecilia's steeple, flashed like sheet lightning through his tortured head. In one sweeping movement he reached for, seized, and hurled this image of his obsession against the far wall, his composure shattering like the glass in the frame. A moan, one in sound not unlike Priscilla's, but one spawned by agony rather than ecstasy, started in his stomach and rose through his throat. "Oh goddamn us!" he cried.

He ran to an outside door and, straining, pitting every ounce of his strength against the wind, forced it open. But it was too dark to see anything outside. The entire neighborhood, like the entire city and surrounding communities—McClellanville, Awendaw, Goose Creek, Monck's Corner, Sullivan's Island, Summerville, the Isle of Palms, Folly Beach, James Island, Hanahan—all were enshrouded in black wind and rain. Visual confirmation of St. Cecilia's share of the catastrophe would have to wait.

With a strong flashlight, Bubba could make out only that the water level had risen to the doorstep, which meant at least half the houses on Meeting, Tradd, Church, Atlantic, Water, and other streets south of Broad were already flooded.

Standing in a puddle of rain water that had immediately formed in the doorway, Bubba pulled the door shut and in a daze walked down the long hall toward a small auxiliary chapel dedicated to St. Thomas.

Under ordinary circumstances, he came to this quiet corner of the church several times a week to pray and meditate. It was while meditating here that he had been inspired to prepare what turned out to be for his congregation one of his most unsettling sermons, for the conservative diocese one of its most controversial, and for himself one of the most fulfilling. He had delivered it the Sunday after Easter:

> . . . The tradition that after the Resurrection in atonement for his doubts, his disbelief, Thomas journeyed to the far reaches of the known world, the Indian subcontinent, to preach the Gospel—this should be an inspiration for us, not only to spread the Good News wherever we may, but also to journey to the far reaches of our own understanding of what the life of our Lord, His Crucifixion, and His Resurrection were all about.
>
> A close examination of the Holy Scriptures fails to reveal any indication to

the effect that Thomas followed through on Jesus' invitation to place a finger and hands in His wounds. There has only been an *assumption* among some of us, which I, personally, would not even elevate to the level of terming it a *tradition*, that Thomas followed through.

Could it be, my friends, that there is an attitude—to coin a term for it, the "Thomas syndrome"—prevalent among Christians which requires us to be convinced by our spiritual advisors and teachers of a *corporeal* Resurrection in order for our faith to be validated?

To paraphrase what the Lord Himself said to Thomas, perhaps we should be told: "Christians, because you have been persuaded by tradition and theology that His human heart began pumping blood again, you have believed. Blessed are they who have not required such persuasion, and yet have believed."

Can it be insignificant that John in his Gospel did not record Thomas putting a finger into the nail wound? In the St. Joseph Daily Missal used by our Catholic brothers and sisters, we read: "St. Thomas doubted the Lord's Resurrection. He was invited by Jesus to place his fingers into His Holy Wounds. Suddenly from incredulity he passed to ardent faith, exclaiming: *My Lord and my God!*" A key word in that quotation might be "suddenly"; otherwise, this learned commentary could have said something like, "Right after Thomas put his finger into the wound . . . ." Whatever Thomas saw, either with his eyes or with his heart, was sufficient to make him a true believer and an extraordinary missionary. To have gone through with the further "proof"

> of fingering bloody tendons, muscles, and so forth, would have been an insult unworthy of any believer.

It was not under ordinary circumstances, however, that Bubba came to the Chapel of St. Thomas on this particular night. Drenched from the moment in the doorway, sodden with self-doubt, he entered and approached the altar. The carpet in the aisle squished from storm water that somehow had seeped in and saturated it. At the altar rail he prostrated himself and vented his guilt and his grief.

* * *

Sweeping in from the sea on the night of September 21, 1989, Hurricane Hugo was the most devastating storm to strike the Carolina coast this century. As merciless as General Sherman's soldiers on their infamous March to the Sea over a hundred years earlier, this aberration of nature damaged or destroyed everything in its path. Neither homes nor schools nor shops nor forests nor churches were spared.

The next day a Charleston newspaper sent a reporter to Mepkin Abbey, a Trappist monastery located about forty miles up the Cooper River in Berkeley County, to check on damage there. After showing him around the Abbey, pointing out acres of twisted trees and devastated buildings—as well as their sacred sculptures which were, perhaps miraculously, unharmed—a monk recited for the reporter Shakespeare's Sonnet LXXIII:

> That time of year thou mayst in me behold
> When yellow leaves, or none, or few, do hang
> Upon those boughs which shake against the cold,
> Bare ruin'd choirs, where late the sweet birds sang.
> In me thou seest the twilight of such day
> As after sunset fadeth in the west,
> Which by and by black night doth take away
> ....

SOUTH CAROLINA STATE LIBRARY
0 01 01 0192663 1